MASS EXTINCTION

Examining the Current Crisis

MASS EXTINCTION

Tricia Andryszewski

TFCB Twenty-First Century Books · Minneapolis

For Matthew and Bridget

Twenty-First Century Books
A division of Lerner Publishing Group, Inc.
241 First Avenue North
Minneapolis, MN 55401 U.S.A.

Website address: www.lernerbooks.com

Library of Congress Cataloging-in-Publication Data

Andryszewski, Tricia, 1956–
    Mass extinction : examining the current crisis / by Tricia Andryszewski.
        p.   cm. — (Discovery!)
    Includes bibliographical references and index.
    ISBN 978-0-8225-7523-8 (lib. bdg. : alk. paper)
    1. Extinction (Biology)—Juvenile literature. I. Title.
QH78.A53 2008
576.8'4—dc22   2007025620

Manufactured in the United States of America
1 2 3 4 5 6 – DP – 13 12 11 10 09 08

CONTENTS

POPPING RIVETS

In the winter, a forest in southern Connecticut can look bottom heavy. Down low, thick evergreen leaves remain on the mountain laurel from last summer. Up above, the tree branches are bare, brown, leafless skeletons. In the summer, the same forest might look top heavy, with most of the greenery high up in the canopy. The leaves up on the trees are by then full size. For a short time each spring, a near perfect balance is struck. An evenly distributed spangling of green shows on herbs and grasses poking out of the brown leaf litter on the ground, on mountain laurel leaves at eye level, and on the young leaves of saplings and mature trees at mid level and canopy.

But something is missing from this forest—something that used to be one of the most beautiful signs of spring. There's not a single dogwood tree. Over the past two decades, dogwoods have disappeared from the understory of hardwood forests from New England to Georgia. Millions of dogwoods have been killed by a fast-spreading fungus. We still see dogwoods blooming in people's yards and along the sides of roads. There, sunshine and air movement discourage the fungus. But back in the woods, their native habitat, they have mainly disappeared.

Flowering dogwood trees in this forest in Georgia (facing page) have a disease that causes them to die back. In the spring, the fungus Discula destructiva *turns the leaves brown and infected twigs are bare (inset). Blossoms will be brown, and the tree may stop blooming entirely. If the fungus spreads to the main stem, or trunk, of the tree, the tree will die.*

Everywhere in this same forest you can hear the sound of many little streams in the springtime. At that time of year, they're filled with snowmelt and spring rain. If you walk here in the evening, you should hear frogs calling. A little later in the summer, you should expect to hear at least one of them kerplunk into a stream. In recent years, though, the number of frogs has been shrinking. This has been happening not only in Connecticut but all around the world. Songbirds, too, are fewer in number than they used to be. Are we heading for the "silent spring" that biologist Rachel Carson warned us about decades ago? The woods have certainly become quieter.

One trail in this Connecticut forest weaves between hemlock trees near a stream running steeply downhill over mossy rocks. It's cool and green there. The ground is soft with a carpet of short, flat hemlock needles. The air smells clean and fresh. It's as though the air has been washed by the tumbling water and filtered by lacy hemlock branches. But the hemlocks may not be around much longer. Hemlock woolly adelgid is infecting the trees near this spot and will probably kill these trees some-day. The adelgid is an imported insect pest that sucks the fluid out of hemlock trees. Adelgids could eventually cause hemlocks to disappear from their native forests everywhere in the eastern United States.

The hemlocks aren't the only tree to be wiped out in this way. The great chestnut blight in the first half of the twentieth century destroyed what was then eastern North America's dominant tree species. (Chestnut trees used to be as common as oaks are in modern times.) The chestnut blight, too, was caused by an imported pest, a disease carried to North America by mistake from overseas. People who grew up during the blight that destroyed the American chestnut trees saw the forest

Hemlocks across eastern North America are threatened by the hemlock woolly adelgid (above). The insect (inset), which is less than 0.06 inch (0.15 centimeter), originated in Asia. The pest has no natural enemies in North America. As the hemlock woolly adelgid matures, it develops a wool-like coating that it uses to protect itself and its eggs.

they had known turn into something different, within decades. The disappearance of the chestnut trees affected other species as well. For each kind of tree shapes the woodland society in which it lives. It colors our experience of the forest, just as the company of a friend colors our experience of anything we do together.

People in the eastern United States are seeing another such change, as the hemlocks die. And, in fact, people in all parts of the world are seeing such changes. Everywhere, many kinds of trees and other plants, animals, birds, and other wildlife are disappearing, in many cases becoming extinct, for many reasons.

SIGNS THAT A SPECIES IS IN DANGER OF EXTINCTION

- Its numbers are dropping sharply, even if those numbers are still large.
- Its range (the area in which it lives) is small and shrinking.
- Its populations (groups of its members living separately) are small, and their numbers are dropping, even if that drop isn't sharp.
- Its numbers are very small, or it is found only in a very small range.

 POPPING RIVETS

A species of plant or animal is said to become extinct when its last living representative dies. Extinction can be either local, such as the dogwoods in the forest described here, or worldwide. In each case, extinction reduces Earth's biological diversity—the complexity and variety of life. The simplest measure of Earth's biological diversity (called biodiversity for short) is the total number of species living on Earth. But this is not the only measure. Biodiversity also shows itself in whole communities of living things uniquely adapted to living together in a particular patch of forest, prairie, or marsh. Individuals that are well suited to that place and community tend to thrive and reproduce better than individuals that are less well suited. As a result, different populations of the same species living in different places develop small but significant differences in their gene

The dodo was a flightless bird that lived on the island of Mauritius in the Indian Ocean. The dodo became extinct in the 1600s after the arrival of Portuguese sailors, who hunted them. The dodo's disappearance led to changes in the entire ecosystem on Mauritius. This print of a dodo appeared in a 1760 publication called Gleanings of Natural History *by George Edwards. The drawing was likely based on a stuffed specimen.*

pools. (A gene pool is the total genetic inheritance of a population that breeds together.) The dogwood trees that used to live in the woods in Connecticut, for example, would have developed a slightly different set of genes than the dogwoods living in a forest in northern Florida.

Loss of genetic diversity through the local extinctions of these slightly different gene pools weakens the entire species. The more genetically alike all the members of a species are, the more susceptible they all might be to a particular disease or disaster. Loss of diversity increases the risk that all of that species—all dogwoods or all hemlocks, for example—will someday become extinct. At the same time, each species extinction, local or global, makes it more likely that other species in the same living community will become extinct also. This is because the extinct species no longer provides food or shelter or meets other needs for the remaining members of its community.

The "rivet-popper" hypothesis was developed in the 1980s by Stanford University biologists Anne and Paul Ehrlich as a way to better understand how this works. According to this hypothesis, each species in any living community (called an ecosystem) helps in some way to keep that living community alive. This works in much the same way that each of the many rivets in an airplane helps hold that plane together. If just one species is lost (or just one rivet pops out of the airplane), the whole ecosystem (or airplane) is weakened. But the whole thing is probably not in danger of falling apart. If more than one species or rivets are lost, the danger increases. Each rivet that pops out of an airplane puts the remaining rivets under increasingly greater strain. In the same way, each lost species weakens its ecosystem more and more, increasing the risk that the whole thing will crash and not recover. Weakened ecosystems are especially at risk for such a crash when faced with an episode of stress that a healthier ecosystem would survive, such as a drought. In the past decade or so, the rivet-popper hypothesis has become more and more widely accepted as a good analogy for the way the world really works.

In the Connecticut woods and in other places all over the world where species have gone extinct, how many "rivets" have popped? Is the "airplane," the whole web of life on Earth, our natural life-support system, about to fall apart? Is it tough enough to weather the kind and amount of species extinctions going on in the twenty-first century? Is it perhaps weaker than we think?

Mass extinction of species is not new to Earth. In fact, scientists have been able to determine that Earth has seen many extinction crises in the distant past. In five of these crises, more than two-thirds of the planet's species died out.

Many scientists believe that Earth is either on the brink of or already well into another such crisis—its sixth great mass extinction. The current extinction crisis, if that's what it is, is the first to have been brought on or at least to have been greatly influenced by human activities.

Are the scientists who believe that most of the planet's species are dying right? Are they wrong? Do we even know enough to answer that question? If not, by the time we do know the answer, will it be too late to do anything about it?

Chapter 1

MASS EXTINCTIONS IN THE PAST

When Earth formed 4.6 billion years ago, it was a ball of hot liquid. The planet became cool enough for living things to develop and survive on it a little less than 4 billion years ago. About 3.75 billion years ago, the first, very simple single-celled forms of life appeared. Somewhat more complex single-cell life first appeared 1.8 billion years ago. Those single cells carried their genetic material much as we humans do, in a specialized part of the cell called the nucleus.

That's about as complicated as life could get at that time. Larger, more complex forms of life require more oxygen than does a small single-cell organism. For a very long time, not enough oxygen was in Earth's air to support multicell organisms. Eventually, though, the amount of oxygen in the air rose from about 1 percent to a level close to the present-day 21 percent. Very soon after that, the first, very simple creatures made up of more than one cell appeared on Earth. That happened about 630 million years ago. More complex multicell life followed about 530 million years ago, in the great expansion of biological diversity known as the Cambrian explosion.

An artist's painting of prehistoric organisms that lived during the Cambrian period (530 to 490 million years ago). During a period known as the Cambrian explosion, the number of new organisms on Earth, many with hard outer bodies, expanded faster and with greater numbers than ever before.

The Cambrian explosion took place in as short a time as five million years, likely no more than ten million years. During this time, all the basic body plans for life-forms found on Earth ever since came into being. Half of these kinds of body plans disappeared in the first of Earth's five great extinction crises, 440 million years ago. No new ones have appeared since. Thirty or so exist in modern times.

BACKGROUND EXTINCTION AND EXTINCTION CRISES

Extinction is one of the most basic facts of life on Earth. Although we don't know for sure, perhaps 30 billion or so species have lived on Earth since the beginning of the Cambrian explosion. If 30 million species exist (a good educated guess), then 99.9 percent of all the species that ever existed have become extinct. Even if the 30 billion/30 million estimates aren't quite right, fossils show that by far most of the species that ever lived on this planet have become extinct. (Fossils are the preserved remains of long-dead creatures, found in stone. Most fossils are from species that no longer exist.)

Extinction doesn't always happen at a steady pace. During most of the history of life on Earth, there has been a relatively steady "background" rate of extinction. When this is going on, species die out here and there, from time to time. The number of species dying out is close to or less than the number of new species arising. But extinction doesn't always happen at a steady pace. It can accelerate during a crisis, such as extreme climate changes. During these times, the number of species becoming extinct has been much greater than the number of new species.

Most (but not all) of these mass extinction crises took place in times when sea levels dropped dramatically. However, at other

 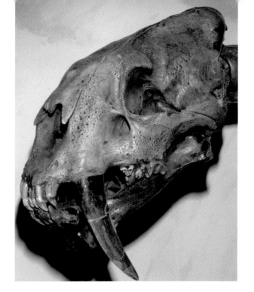

Fossils, such as this ancient plant (left) *and sabertooth tiger scull* (right), *give scientists clues about life hundreds of millions of years ago.*

times when the planet's oceans were very low, mass extinction didn't happen. So other reasons must be at work as well. Likewise, the periods of global cooling we call ice ages have sometimes but not always gone hand in hand with mass extinction.

A few dozen of the planet's mass extinction crises have been less severe than the others. These moderate crises killed off 15 to 40 percent of marine (ocean-dwelling) species living at the time. (The fossil record for marine species is much more complete than for land animals. This is because nearly all land animals die in conditions that don't make for good fossils. Still, scientists have found evidence that each of these extinction crises had catastrophic effects on land animals as well as marine species.)

THE BIG FIVE

Five great extinction crises—the Big Five—weren't moderate at all. Each of these crises killed two-thirds or more of the species then living on Earth.

This extinct armored fish of the genus Dinichthys *lived during the late Devonian period. A mass extinction wiped out this and most other species but made way for the rapid expansion of other species who survived the extinction crisis.*

END-ORDOVICIAN CRISIS This was the crash at the end of the Cambrian explosion, 440 million years ago. Following this great crash, no new kinds of basic body plans for living creatures arose. But a burst of new species within the surviving kinds of body plans pumped up biological diversity to nearly where it was before the crash. This biodiversity persisted, more or less, for nearly 200 million years.

LATE DEVONIAN CRISIS This crisis took place 365 million years ago. After it was over, many species of reptiles took advantage of the food and habitat opportunities opened by the extinction of other forms of life. They thrived for more than 100 million years.

END-PERMIAN CRISIS This crisis, about 250 million years ago, was the worst of the Big Five. Perhaps 95 percent of all

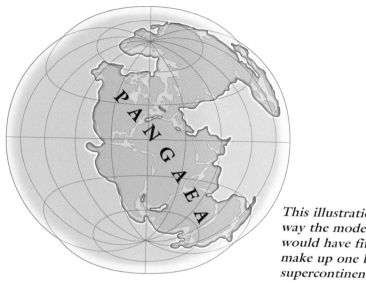

This illustration shows the way the modern continents would have fit together to make up one big supercontinent called Pangaea.

species then living on Earth became extinct. We don't know for sure what caused the end-Permian crisis. But recent scientific research suggests that climate change brought about by geological change might have done it. Long ago, all the world's continents were clumped together into one huge landmass, known as Pangaea. Pangaea eventually broke apart, and this rearrangement of landmasses lowered sea levels. The lower sea levels, in turn, exposed to air the decaying remains of long-dead plants and animals once buried deep in the ocean. Exposure to air sped up the decay. Decay uses oxygen, and all that rot could have reduced the level of oxygen from about 21 percent (close to the present level) to perhaps 16 percent or even lower. This level of oxygen would have been low enough to stress or kill animal life. Meanwhile, Pangaea's breakup might also have set off volcanic eruptions. Such volcanoes could have released enough carbon dioxide to create a greenhouse effect, with the carbon dioxide trapping heat much as the windows of a closed-up car do on sunny days. This would have raised temperatures all over the world enough to stress or kill plants as well as animals.

The loss of life in the end-Permian crisis was great. Just as great was the ecological opportunity it presented. The end-Permian crisis nearly extinguished the reptiles that thrived after the late-Devonian crisis. This opened opportunities for the dinosaurs that were then able to dominate Earth's dry land for 140 million years. New species arose, more and more of them.

The end-Permian crisis wiped out many species, leaving the way clear for new species such as dinosaurs to establish themselves and thrive.

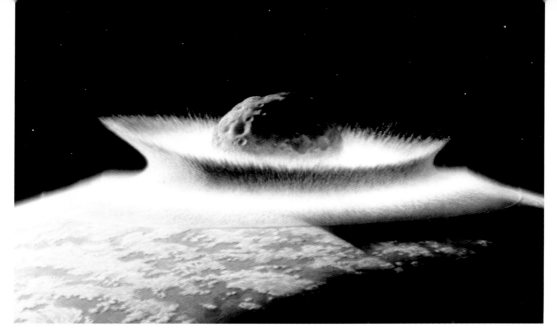

An artist's impression of the impact a huge asteroid would have made on Earth. Many scientists think that just such an event may have ended the Cretaceous period, making way for mammals to become the dominant creatures on Earth.

END-TRIASSIC CRISIS This sharp setback, 210 million years ago, checked but didn't end the rapid growth in new species begun after the end-Permian crisis. After the end-Triassic crisis, the fast pace of species creation resumed. Within 100 million years, biological diversity (as measured by the number of families of species) surpassed the high point of the Cambrian explosion.

END-CRETACEOUS CRISIS The most likely cause of this crisis was the impact of a huge asteroid hitting Earth 65 million years ago. The impact threw enough dust and debris high into the atmosphere to block out sunlight long enough to kill most plant life. (Scientists have identified a large enough impact crater of the right age underlying the surface of the Yucatán Peninsula in Mexico. Other, smaller craters made at about the same time have been found around the world. This indicates that Earth probably passed through a whole shower of meteors at that time.) Without plants to eat, most animals died as well. Among those that died were all the dinosaurs except for those whose descendants eventually evolved into modern birds.

While reptiles in the form of dinosaurs had dominated Earth's dry land, mammals were small, weak, and few in number. (Their small size probably helped them to survive the extinction crisis that killed the dinosaurs. Larger animals tend to be more vulnerable to environmental stresses.) The end of the dinosaurs freed resources the dinosaurs had previously consumed. Mammals took advantage of this. They increased in kind, size, and number. They became the new dominant creatures on Earth.

BAD LUCK OR BAD GENES?

Since the 1970s, scientific opinion has moved toward the idea that extinction occurs as a result of a combination of bad genes and bad luck. Most background extinctions and extinctions during the lesser, moderate extinction crises have probably been due more to genes. The species that went extinct in those times were likely somehow less genetically fit than their neighbors that survived. The evolutionary process of natural selection first identified by Darwin in the 1800s rules during normal times. The species that survive background extinction tend to do so because they're better fitted for survival in their environments.

The Big Five extinction crises, though, involved a very large component of bad luck. Extreme conditions occur so very rarely that most species appear, live for millions of years, and then die out for other reasons. Species that die because they encounter such extreme conditions are simply unlucky. Natural selection has never screened their genes for fitness to deal with

the unusual environmental conditions that occur in major extinction crises. Being well suited for such previously unknown conditions is a lucky accident, not a result of natural selection. As a species, dinosaurs had never seen conditions like those in the crisis in which they became extinct. The ancestors of the mammals that lived with the dinosaurs had no experience with such conditions, either. It was just luck that the mammals happened to be better able to survive those conditions.

Nor, as we shall see, has natural selection "fitted" modern species to deal with the stresses that humans have introduced to their environments. Extinction or survival in current times, as during the Big Five crises, appears to be more and more a matter of luck.

Chapter 2

THE HUMAN INFLUENCE

Humans didn't experience any of the Big Five extinction crises. We first appeared on Earth long after those events were over. Humans did, however, participate in a moderate extinction crisis at the end of the most recent ice age (1.8 million to 11,000 years ago). We did this by hunting and killing large numbers of big, cold-adapted animals. These animals were already struggling to adapt to the warming climate. Many species did not survive the double whammy of climate change and hunting by humans.

Here's how that happened. By about fifty thousand years ago, humans were migrating out of their tropical ancestral home in Africa. In colder places, they found both hardship (cold weather) and new resources. Among those resources were large animals previously unknown to humans. (Colder places tend to have larger animals, since big body size helps an animal get through cold winters.) Bigger game animals were a big help to these early humans, who depended on hunting for much or most of their food. When they encountered megafauna (large animals) that had never before seen humans, the animals didn't know to be afraid of them. When these members of the elephant family ignored human newcomers, humans killed the unwary beasts and feasted.

In this artist's impression, hunters attack a group of mammoths. Mammoths were large elephant-like creatures that were adapted for living in cold climates during Earth's last ice age. A warming global climate and hunting by humans probably led to the extinction of the species.

From Australia to the Americas, dozens of species of megafauna died out and became extinct not long after the first humans arrived among them. Australia and New Guinea had giant kangaroos. They also had giant marsupials that looked like rhinoceroses; a species of 400-pound (180-kilogram) birds (too heavy to fly, thus easy to hunt); giant lizards and snakes; and crocodiles. All of these creatures began to go extinct as humans began to live among them. All were gone forever by thirty-five thousand years ago.

A similar story played out in the Americas but later. Humans didn't arrive there until near the end of the last ice age, perhaps twelve thousand years ago. When humans did arrive, they found American versions of elephants, horses, lions, cheetahs,

This illustration shows many of the mammals and birds that lived in North America during the Pleistocene epoch (1.8 million to 11,000 years ago). The creatures shown here include giant ground sloths, ancient bison, dire wolves, and early horses.

camels, and giant sloths on North America's Great Plains. All were extinct by ten thousand years ago. More large-mammal extinctions took place in the Americas in just those two thousand years than all that had happened there in the preceding two million years.

Did early human hunters kill them off? Probably human hunting was one of several reasons for these megafauna extinctions. During the tens of thousands of years when humans were first spreading out around the planet, Earth's climate went through changes that made it harder for large animals to survive. Large animals need a lot of food. Climate change can make food supplies unreliable. Probably diseases carried by humans (and by the animals that traveled with us) killed more animals than human hunters did.

IMPACT OF AGRICULTURE AND CIVILIZATION

The megafauna extinction is just part of a much bigger story of human impact on species extinction. All over the world, from the first humans in Africa to all of us in modern times, people have adapted to their environment. But we've also changed our environments to make them more suitable to our needs. Some species have adapted well to the changes humans have made. But many have not.

Human impact on nature has grown as our population has grown. Up to about twelve thousand years ago, the total number of humans on Earth was probably not more than five million. Then a new way of life, agriculture, made it possible to feed more people than could be fed by ancient methods of hunting and gathering. By seven thousand years ago, humans were becoming farmers in more and more places around the world. With more food, our numbers were growing. By then we numbered perhaps ten million. Wherever agriculture was adopted, both our growing numbers and the changes we made to the land gave wildlife fewer places to live and eventually drove many species to extinction. In the Nile Valley in Egypt, for example, elephants, rhinoceroses, and giraffes had become locally extinct by five thousand years ago. They have never returned to that part of their previous range. The aurochs (a forest-dwelling ancestor of modern cattle) became extinct in Britain four thousand years ago. It slowly disappeared from the rest of Europe as well, as forest was turned into farmland.

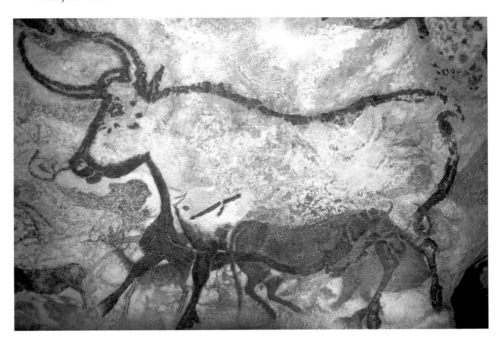

A cave painting from the Lascaux cave in southwestern France depicts the cowlike auroch. Early cavemen living in Europe encountered this animal. It became extinct thousands of years ago.

By two thousand years ago, the innovations of early civilization had allowed the human population of the planet to soar to 300 million. The development of empires with wider, ultimately global reach brought the world's population to 1 billion early in the nineteenth century. Then the development of industry and the harnessing of fossil fuels such as coal drove another surge in population. By 1950 the world's population was roughly 2.5 billion. Since then, in just half a century, our population has soared to more than 6 billion. And it's still climbing.

ACCELERATING EXTINCTIONS

Only in the past century or so have we done much research into the human impact on species extinction. Clearly, human impact has grown right along with not only our increasing numbers but also our increasing power over nature.

Estimates of past and present extinction rates vary a lot. One scientific expert will make different choices than another about which assumptions and guesses to use in fleshing out and making sense of incomplete data. So the conclusions different experts come to will be different as well. And the data we have about nature and human effects on nature is far from complete. We don't, for example, have a reliable, agreed-upon head count for the total number of species living in the world. We certainly don't have such a count for the number living at any time in the past.

Some scientists believe that human activities have had a significant impact on overall extinction rates for thousands of years. It's hard to say if our impact was really great enough to drive extinction rates beyond the normal range of background extinction. Our knowledge of the biodiversity that existed thousands of years ago is just inadequate.

HENRY DAVID THOREAU ON EXTINCTION

Concern about species extinctions caused by humans is more widely

shared than it used to be. But it isn't completely new.

"When I think," the American naturalist Henry David Thoreau *(left)* wrote in his journal a century and a half ago, "what were the various sounds and notes, the migrations and works, and changes of fur and plumage which ushered in the spring and marked the other seasons of the year, I am reminded that this my life in nature, this particular round of natural phenomena which I call a year, is lamentably incomplete. . . . I take infinite pains to know all the phenomena of the spring, for instance, thinking that I have here the entire poem, and then, to my chagrin, I hear that it is but an imperfect copy that I possess and have read, that my ancestors have torn out many of the first leaves and grandest passages, and mutilated it in many places. I should not like to think that some demigod had come before me and picked out some of the best of the stars. I wish to know an entire heaven and an entire earth."

—*Henry David Thoreau's journal, 1865*

Clearly, though, from prehistory to the present, humans have at least had a significant impact on the extinctions of certain kinds of species. We know that certain species of mammals and birds no longer exist because of human hunting or other actions. And our knowledge of mammals and birds is much more complete than our knowledge of, say, species of fungi. We know enough to be pretty sure that human activities have driven extinction of mammals and birds to rates well above the background extinction rate. We also know that this has been going on for thousands of years, at least since the megafauna extinctions. Clearly, the rate of extinction of these creatures is accelerating. One respected accounting says that between the years 1600 and 1900, an average of about one species of mammal or bird became extinct every four years. Then, in the twentieth century, that extinction rate jumped to one each year. That's a rate comparable to the extinction rates of past mass extinctions.

Experts disagree about the overall numbers and rates of species extinction. But most agree that extinction is increasing sharply. For example, one expert might estimate that a quarter century ago, one hundred species of all sorts (from plants and animals to bacteria and fungi) became extinct each year. The same expert might say that, in the twenty-first century, perhaps one hundred become extinct each day. Another expert might define the normal background extinction rate at one to ten species per year. That expert might estimate that the current extinction rate is at least one thousand species per year.

Chapter 3

ALTERED HABITATS

Humans alter natural habitat when they develop industry. They alter still more habitat when they convert wild land to pastures and fields. And they alter even more natural habitat to build towns, cities, and suburbs and the roads that link them. All this activity increases as human population grows. Earth's human population in the past century has exploded. Some scientists believe that human alteration and destruction of natural habitat could, in just the next few years or decades, drive the world's extinction rate to as many as one hundred thousand species each year. Even scientists who believe that number is too high generally agree that habitat alteration is the greatest force driving extinction in the twenty-first century.

HABITAT ALTERATION IN THE WORLD'S TEMPERATE ZONES

About one-third of all the land on Earth that's fit for human habitation (land that's not covered by bare rock, ice, or blowing sand) can currently be described as "highly disturbed" by humans. Much of this land has been plowed for farming or grazed so heavily by livestock that much of its natural plant life is gone. Still more has been paved over for cities, roads, and other modern infrastructure. Most "highly disturbed" land is in the world's temperate climate zones. (The temperate zones are in between the hot tropics near the equator and the frigid arctic zones near the poles.) Most of this land is suitable for farming, convenient for urban centers, or near rivers and oceans.

In addition, much of the world's remaining habitable land can be described as "partly disturbed." This is true for both temperate and tropical places. Most of this "partly disturbed" land is young forest that's less biologically diverse than the old-growth forests that have been cut down. (Such young forests tend to have fewer tree species and fewer wildflowers, for example.) Even counting this younger, less diverse forest, the world has no more than half the forests it had eight thousand years ago.

The altering of natural habitat for human use began thousands of years ago. It has greatly accelerated in the past 150 years. This has happened in step with population growth and new technologies to harness the power of fossil fuels.

Slash pine tree farms, such as this one in Apalachicola National Forest in Florida, are much less biodiverse than the native forests they replace. Slash pines, which have a rapid growth rate, are frequently planted to supply pulp for the paper industry. But the loss of biodiversity in younger forests like this could have devastating effects.

Sawmills like this one on the Penobscot River in Maine in the mid-1800s turned thousands of trees into boards to be used in building.

We can see this acceleration clearly in the history of human alteration of natural habitat in the United States. When the first Europeans landed in America, a thick forest covered the eastern part of the continent. This forest stretched from the Atlantic Ocean to the edge of the Great Plains. By 1800 much of New England's forest had already been cut down. This was done mostly to clear land for farming and partly to provide wood for fuel and lumber for building. Also by 1800, most of the rivers and streams in New England and near the Atlantic coast had been dammed to create hydropower to turn mills. Populations of many species of plants and animals that depend on healthy forests and free-flowing streams dropped sharply.

North America's population of European immigrants and their descendants grew rapidly. They pressed farther west. As they moved on, they left behind devastation—worn-out fields, forests stripped of their trees, and streams and rivers choked with eroded topsoil.

Cutting the forest freed land for farming. But it also had unintentional side effects. The exposed soil became drier. Unprotected by forest cover, the soil baked hotter in the summer and was more likely to freeze deeply in the winter. Thus it was less able to hold water in either season. More water running off this soil (instead of soaking in) meant that flooding became more sudden and serious. Rain washed exposed soil away into streams and lakes. Streams and lakes filled up with silt, sometimes turning into swamps. This runoff into streams also killed fish and other species that depend on clear running water. Species of wildlife that depend on healthy forest, river, lake, and wetlands habitats disappeared. All of these habitats saw sharp drops in biodiversity as the land was altered for human uses.

Some of the crops grown on much of this altered land were especially damaging to the soil. Much of the damage came from depletion of the soil by growing one crop over and over again, because it was the most valuable at the market. Tobacco and cotton in the Chesapeake Bay region and in the South are

Crops such as tobacco (below) *and cotton were highly valued as cash crops in the southern United States.*

good examples of this. In other places, steep lands that had been cleared of trees and plowed soon eroded to rocky infertility. You can still see such damage from generations ago in northern New England and in the Appalachian Mountains and nearby hilly country.

Beginning in the early nineteenth century, farmers began to abandon millions of acres (hectares) of worn-out farmland in the eastern United States. This happened even as new farmland was being made from newly cleared forest nearby. The abandoned farmland, in time, became young forest. This partly disturbed habitat grew in altered conditions on depleted soil, so it was less biologically diverse than the forest that had been there previously.

Meanwhile, whatever forest remained was cleared faster and faster in the nineteenth century. In the middle of that century, the lumber industry introduced the circular saw and steam-powered sawmills. By 1900 little of the United States' eastern forest remained.

By then westward-moving farmers had plowed much of the western United States' prairie habitat. Many believed that the deep, rich prairie soil would yield ever-larger crops of grain for generations to come. That dream ended in the 1930s dust bowl. In that disaster, millions of tons of prairie topsoil blew away after years of careless farming. In modern times, nearly all the Great Plains' former tallgrass prairie habitat is plowed cropland. Most of this land is devoted to corn and soybeans. The drier mixed-grass and short-grass prairie farther west has become cropland and pasture for cattle. Here, too, native species have been pushed aside and have become extinct or nearly so across much of their former range.

In the United States, most new habitat alteration takes one of two forms. Natural forests are totally cleared and replaced

A dust storm in 1937 approached houses in the midwestern United States. Years of overplanting combined with severe drought left topsoil extremely dry. Large windstorms carried away the topsoil in the form of dust storms.

with less diverse tree farms. In other places, urban sprawl turns farmland or partly disturbed forest into homes, office buildings, stores, and roads. In the next few decades, most urban sprawl is expected to take place around a few dozen big-city areas. Hundreds of endangered species live only in those areas about to be developed.

IN THE TROPICS

Most of the natural habitat on lands that humans can inhabit in the world's temperate zones has already been altered for human uses. Further alteration to that land continues to cause species extinctions and reduce biodiversity. But this is on habitat that's already been altered. In the twenty-first century, most of the places where undisturbed natural habitat is being first put to human use are concentrated in the tropics, especially in tropical forests.

There's more biodiversity, more species per acre typically, in the tropical zone near the equator. There's less biodiversity in temperate zones. There's less still near the poles. This means that destroying a patch of habitat in the tropics can affect ten times as many species, or more, compared to destroying a same-sized patch of temperate forest. Tropical rain forests cover only a small fraction of the world's land. But they support more than half the world's species. Other tropical habitats are also typically richer in species than are temperate and arctic habitats.

Worldwide, forest loss is rapidly accelerating. In the 1990s, about 80,000 square miles (208,000 sq. kilometers) of forest were lost each year. This was up sharply from just a decade earlier. Forest destruction is concentrated in the tropical and near-

Tropical rain forests are dense with millions of species of plants, animals, insects, fungi, bacteria, and more. Many species have yet to be discovered.

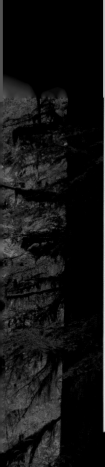

BIODIVERSITY

Biological diversity "can be eroded away fragment by fragment, and irreversibly so if the abnormal stress is unrelieved. This vulnerability stems from life's composition as swarms of species of limited geographical distribution. Every habitat, from Brazilian rain forest to Antarctic Bay to thermal vent, harbors a unique combination of plants and animals. Each kind of plant and animal living there is linked in the food web to only a small part of the other species. Eliminate one species, and another increases in number to take its place. Eliminate a great many species, and the local ecosystem starts to decay visibly. Productivity drops as the channels of the nutrient cycles are clogged. More of the biomass is sequestered in the form of dead vegetation and slowly metabolizing, oxygen-starved mud, or is simply washed away. Less competent pollinators take over as the best-adapted bees, moths, birds, bats, and other specialists drop out. Fewer seeds fall, fewer seedlings sprout. Herbivores decline, and their predators die away in close concert."

—*American biologist Edward O. Wilson*, The Diversity of Life, *1992*

tropical parts of the world. Here poverty and population growth are both most extreme. And forest species diversity is highest. In most of these places, we're unlikely even to identify the full range of that diversity before it's lost. On the large tropical island of Borneo, for example, forest is fast being lost to expanding rubber and palm plantations. Researchers there have found more than 360 new species just since 1994, including an elusive catlike carnivore discovered in 2005. In recent years, the regions of the world with the highest rates of forest destruction have been Africa and the Caribbean.

Stuart Pimm, shown here with a lemur, is a professor at Duke University in Durham, North Carolina. He studies the effects of habitat loss and species extinction.

THE HUMPTY DUMPTY EFFECT

Once a habitat has been substantially altered, reintroducing the same species to the same place won't re-create the ecological community that once lived there. Ecological communities evolve together over time. Even if you know and can gather all the species that ought to be found in a certain ecosystem, it's not possible to re-create one from scratch.

Scientist Stuart Pimm calls this the Humpty Dumpty effect. The effect has been demonstrated both mathematically (with computer models) and in real life. In certain places where natural habitat has been much altered (some parts of the American prairie, for example), there's a good historical record of what species used to live there before the habitat was altered. But when ecologists have gathered the right species and reintroduced them to places where they formerly lived, it hasn't worked out as expected. (Efforts to restore patches of natural habitat take place all the time, from forests and wetlands in Florida, to midwestern prairie, to mountain meadows in the West.) Key species that once thrived in the environment fail to reestablish themselves. Others use up more than their past share of the system's resources. The system just doesn't work the way it used to. Typically, it's less stable than a natural system that has evolved over time. It's also more vulnerable to invasion by nonnative species. And it's less likely to survive periods of environmental stress.

HOT SPOTS

So science as well as common sense tells us that protecting intact, natural ecosystems is the way to go. Protection is far more likely to be successful in sustaining biodiversity than trying to reassemble ecosystems after they're gone or badly damaged.

In recent years, the concept of biodiversity "hot spots" has been promoted as a way to direct conservation efforts toward places where they can have the greatest impact. A biodiversity hot spot is a place that supports an unusually rich concentration of diverse species. Hot spots are especially rich in endemic species (ones found nowhere else). Ecologists have identified thirty-four such hot spots, which together take up about 2 percent of Earth's land. (Hot spots are concentrated in the tropics but found all over the world, from the Caribbean Islands to the coastal forests of eastern Africa to the mountains of central Asia. Hot spots in North America include the California floristic province, home to the giant sequoia; and parts of the Madrean pine-oak woodlands, a type of mountain forest found only in Mexico and on isolated mountaintops in the southwestern United States.) These areas contain approximately half of the world's known endemic species of plants. These reservoirs of unique plants and animals are also reservoirs of unusually rich nonendemic biodiversity. All the hot spots are threatened by human activities that alter habitat.

Chapter 4

KILLING ON PURPOSE

Over the past few centuries, extensive hunting and trapping have had a big impact on reducing the world's wildlife population. Birds, the larger mammals, and fur-bearing and game animals have been especially hard hit. Many have become extinct over vast stretches of their original ranges. (Most of the forests of Appalachia in the eastern United States, for example, have only two large native mammals left—white-tailed deer and black bears. In the past, elk, woodland bison, cougars, and wolves lived there as well.) Some have become extinct entirely.

KILLING OF NORTH AMERICAN WILDLIFE

In North America, the hunting to local extinction of fur-bearing animals is an example of the impact of purposely killing wildlife. Other examples are the Great Plains bison, the passenger pigeon, and grizzly bears and other top predators.

The fur trade was one of the strongest moneymaking motives for Europeans first coming to North America. By the seventeenth century, Europe's fur-bearing wild animals—bears, beavers, and others, even a European species of bison—were nearly all gone. But Europe's marketplace demanded more

European traders at Fort Michilimackinac in Michigan traded manufactured goods for furs with the local Native American population in the eighteenth and nineteenth centuries.

furs. In North America, trappers found plenty of fur. The trappers usually took all the wildlife in one area. Then they moved on to another and then another. Beavers were especially prized for their fur—mostly used to make fancy hats. Beavers were once plentiful from coast to coast. By 1800 they had been hunted just about to extinction everywhere east of the Mississippi River. The trappers moved westward. Fur was one of the few goods valuable enough to take out of remote wilderness by canoes. Great fortunes were made in furs. The richest man of his day in the United States, John Jacob Astor, derived his wealth from beaver pelts. The western fur trade peaked in the 1820s. So many animals were killed so quickly that few remained by the mid-nineteenth century. The fur trade and the American wildlife population never fully recovered.

The great herds of American bison were also hunted near to extinction in the nineteenth century. Their skins were valuable.

A herd of American bison grazes in Custer State Park in South Dakota. Huge herds of bison used to roam the Great Plains of North America. Humans valued them for their hides and meat and hunted them to near extinction in the late 1800s.

But so was the land they grazed on. Farmers wanted to plow the bison's prairie habitat and plant it with grain. Ranchers wanted to graze cattle on it. Killing the bison made the bison's habitat available for farmers and ranchers. At the height of the slaughter, in the 1870s, as many as one million bison were killed each year. By the mid-1880s, only a few hundred remained of the sixty million or more that once roamed the Great Plains. The entire web of native plains wildlife, from dung beetles that lived in bison droppings, to wildflowers whose seeds the bison spread, to wolves and cougars who preyed on young and weak bison, was hit hard by the loss of the bison. The Great Plains' quantity and diversity of life diminished. To take just one example, consider the grizzly bear. Grizzlies once roamed the entire Great Plains. Much of their diet there was bison. With the bison gone, the great bears had little to eat. At the same time, humans with guns were hunting and killing the bears. Grizzly bears withdrew to remote places in the Rockies. Only a tiny fraction of their former population survives, living on a tiny fraction of their former range.

Big predators such as grizzly bears, cougars, and wolves are markers for intact ecology and biodiversity. Where they're present, so usually is a complete set of diverse species. That "complete set" is typically the most life that can in the long run flourish in that particular place. The big predators' killing of other animals helps keep their home habitat healthy in many ways, most obviously by culling the weak and helping to keep plant eaters' populations in balance with wild plant life. We've exterminated most of these predators in places where they pose a danger or economic threat to us. This is why most of the United States has no cougars, wolves, or grizzly bears. All are locally extinct throughout nearly all of their former range.

This print of a male and a female passenger pigeon appears in John James Audubon's Birds of America. *They were once abundant throughout North America until they were hunted into extinction by European settlers in the late 1800s.*

Even more numerous than the great herds of bison were America's once-great flocks of birds. The greatest of these flocks were the passenger pigeons. Likely five billion of them filled the skies when the first Europeans arrived in North America. They represented about one-third of America's bird population at the time. Easy to kill and delicious to eat, passenger pigeons were hunted enthusiastically by Native Americans. Later, passenger pigeons were hunted in even larger numbers by European Americans with guns. Even so, as late as the mid-nineteenth century, several billion of the birds still lived. Most of those birds nested in the Great Lakes region. Then newly laid railroads made it possible for people in that region to send goods for sale to the growing cities of the Northeast. Most of the remaining birds were killed in the 1860s and 1870s. In 1869 Van Buren County, Michigan, alone sent 7.5 million birds to market in the East. The last wild birds were gone by 1900. The very last passenger pigeon died, in a zoo, in 1914.

KILLING OF FISH

Centuries of heavy fishing have brought the decline or collapse of many of the world's most productive fisheries. (A fishery is the harvesting of a particular species of fish from a particular place, such as oysters from the Chesapeake Bay.) The decline continues. Most saltwater fish species currently threatened with extinction are still being fished out faster than their natural rates of reproduction can replace them. In addition, species not yet considered in danger of extinction are being fished out in numbers that will soon threaten them with extinction.

Habitat alteration, mostly from pollution, also contributes to the decline of many species of fish. This is true for both freshwater and saltwater fish. Freshwater biodiversity hot spots harmed by habitat alteration and overfishing include large rivers all over the world, from the Missouri in the United States to the Yangtze in China. Some isolated large lakes are also threatened. Isolated bodies of water often have fish found nowhere else. Saltwater biodiversity hot spots under similar pressures include coral reefs and estuaries and other shallow places near shore.

The water off Cape Cod in Massachusetts is one such watery place harmed by both habitat alteration and overfishing. The collapse of the once-rich fisheries off Cape Cod has occurred over just the past half century. "When I was young," marine biologist and Provincetown, Massachusetts, native Charles "Stormy" Mayo says, "we had a harbor full of boats, and it was no trouble getting lots of fish. I think if we were here in the spring before Europeans arrived, we would have stood on the shore and been amazed at the amount of life that would have suddenly come in with spring's arrival." And what do fishers catch now? "Hardly any codfish that are worth anything. Hardly any haddock. I can't believe that dogfish, which for most of my life has been the bane of fishing around here, is now so depleted that they're regulating to protect it. My grandfather would have said: 'Let them all go, let 'em die, we don't want any more!'"

Farther south, in the Chesapeake Bay, a similar decline and collapse has happened. There, the fish species are different. But the extinction story is much the same. Fish populations naturally ebb and flow, for reasons we don't completely understand. In this way, the blue crabs of the Chesapeake Bay are even more

A MARINE BIOLOGIST COMMENTS ON EXTINCTION

Dr. Charles Mayo points out that the reasons for saving the North Atlantic right whale are complex.

"The extinction of the [North Atlantic] right whale means different things to different people . . . on one level the issue is the protection of the diversity of life within ecosystems.

"On a second level there is that sense of responsibility that many feel for the decline of a species as a result of human activities. . . . Today, entanglement in the ropes and nets of commercial fishing gear and the collision of ships with whales appear to be the principal causes of mortality.

"And this is a time, a day and age when economic health is the paramount rationale for some conservation efforts. Saving whales for economic gain does not seem like an argument that makes much sense, not today. The impetus for protection of the species comes from our belief in the richness of life and the uniqueness of such a special creature, not because someone will make money if they are saved."

—Charles "Stormy" Mayo, 2005

The blue crab (left) feeds on a variety of live and dead fish, crabs, clams, snails, eelgrass, sea lettuce, and decayed vegetation. It is a popular seafood item in the Atlantic region. Overfishing and environmental damage could be having an effect on the blue crab's survival as a species.

mysterious than most other fish. In recent years, the number of crabs there has apparently fallen. It's not clear how much this reduction has to do with overfishing. We also don't know how much it has to do with habitat changes from development near shore, with pollution, or with natural ups and downs. However, crabs are the last remaining major fishery in the bay. Oysters have already been made nearly extinct in the bay by overfishing and pollution. The once-plentiful springtime runs of sturgeon, shad, and other fish are gone as well. In the twenty-first century, few of those who fish on the bay make much money from anything but crabbing. If the crabs go the way of the bay's other fish, no large commercial fishery will be left there at all.

 ## WHALES AND OTHER MARINE MAMMALS

Stormy Mayo's professional specialty is a species on the brink of extinction, the North Atlantic right whale. Its numbers were

This rare shot of a North American right whale was photographed off the coast of Cape Cod, Massachusetts. The view shown here is of the top of the whale's head and jaw.

reduced by hunting, mostly in the nineteenth century, to a small fraction of what they once were. As a result, even long after the hunting stopped, the species' risk of extinction remains high. Its reduced numbers make it vulnerable to both natural and human-created environmental stresses. Only about 350 or so North Atlantic right whales are alive. Nor is the right whale alone in its plight. About one-third of all whale species are currently threatened with extinction. Seals and other marine mammals are also endangered because so many have been killed in the past. Greatly reducing the numbers of any species makes it more vulnerable to normal environmental stresses that a larger population would have a better chance of surviving. Disease, bad weather, or a single season's local failure of an important food source can easily wipe out a small group. In the same situation, at least some of a larger, more widespread population would survive. Greatly reducing the numbers of a species also reduces its genetic diversity and robustness. For example, what happens if all the individuals that have inherited a resistance to a certain disease happen to be killed by hunters? In the future, all members of that species (the descendants of those that survived the hunters) will be vulnerable to that disease. In some cases, reducing a species to very low numbers results in such a concentration of genetic defects that the animals have difficulty reproducing successfully. Some scientists believe that the surviving North Atlantic right whales may be suffering from such reproductive problems.

In addition, any species with greatly reduced numbers suffers from increased vulnerability to human-created stresses. Losing even a few members of a species reduced to only a few hundred makes extinction easier and more likely. This is especially true for long-lived, slow-reproducing species such as whales. For example, whales and other marine mammals often die from entanglement with fishing gear or collisions with ships. If only three or four North Atlantic right whales die this way in a year, that's about 1 percent of the entire species. In 2006 at least six North Atlantic right whales died this way. The whales don't reproduce fast enough to make up for that.

KILLING FOR MARKET

The megafauna extinction thousands of years ago was exceptional. It's unusual for subsistence hunting to drive any species to extinction. (Subsistence hunting provides food or clothing for the hunter, not a surplus to sell.) That kind of killing is limited by how much the hunters and their families and friends can eat or wear. Killing to sell all or part of the dead animal at a market has no such limit. The more people and places a hunter or fisher can sell to, the more creatures it pays to kill. Long-distance transportation and large, far-reaching markets can together suck much more life out of a place than just a local market can. The beavers, bison, passenger pigeons, fish, and whales driven to extinction or near extinction all were killed to meet the demands of large, distant markets.

We no longer hunt North Atlantic right whales. But many other species are being hunted to or near extinction to be sold in the global marketplace. Walk into nearly any fish market, and you'll see species for sale that are being taken from the ocean faster than their remaining members' reproduction can replace them. On the Internet, endangered species are sold illegally to eager buyers all over the world.

Perhaps the greatest risks of hunting to extinction in the twenty-first century are found where species are also threatened by habitat alteration. For example, in previously isolated parts of the world, tropical forests are being cut. Roads built to haul out the cut timber also link these places to regional or global marketplaces for meat, live animals, skins, and horns. The large and growing market for traditional Chinese medicines requires certain animals' bones, horns, and internal organs. This demand may drive tigers, rhinoceroses, and some species of bears to extinction within the next few decades.

Chapter 5

ALIEN INVADERS

At 6,053 feet (1,845 meters), the Richland Balsam Overlook in western North Carolina is the highest point on the Blue Ridge Parkway. It's so high there that the treetops rake mist out of clouds whooshing by. This place once offered a glorious view of a spruce-fir forest. The mountainsides still bristle with the expected spruces. But the only firs you'll see are thousands of silvery dead skeletons reaching up into the clouds. They've been dead so many years that the wind has stripped off all their bark and small brittle twigs. All that's left are their larger branches, bleached by the sun.

It's very sad—and it was all an accident. A century ago, shippers unwittingly brought balsam woolly adelgid over the Atlantic Ocean from Europe. This insect immediately began to spread through northern balsam fir forests. By the 1950s, they had reached the southern Appalachians. During millions of years of evolution, American firs had never before encountered these exotic pests. So they had developed no way to survive their attack. The skeletons you can see along the Blue Ridge Parkway are the remains of Fraser firs killed by adelgids around the 1970s.

Of course, the balsam woolly adelgid isn't the only exotic pest we've introduced to North Carolina's mountains. An imported disease has destroyed the chestnut trees. Dogwood anthracnose, the same fungus that did in the dogwood trees in Connecticut's forests, has been spreading down the Appalachian Mountains since the 1980s. Gypsy moths, hemlock

Gypsy moth caterpillars, such as this one, nibble on the leaves of hardwood trees throughout the eastern United States. The gypsy moth is not a native insect. It was introduced into the United States in 1869 by a French scientist living in Massachusetts.

woolly adelgids, and many other invaders we've introduced to America threaten the forests there too.

EXOTIC INVASIVES

An exotic, or alien, species is one that doesn't naturally occur in a particular place. Instead, it evolved elsewhere and was brought, intentionally or not, to new habitat by humans. Not all exotics take hold and do well in new places: Tropical plants and animals won't survive cold winters. Water lovers won't survive in a desert. An invasive species is one that adapts very well to a new location and takes over habitat and resources that native species previously used. Exotic invasives can thus drive native plant and animal life to extinction. The organisms that have caused the chestnut, fir, hemlock, and dogwood blights are all exotic invasives.

Humans can be seen as the ultimate exotic invasive species. We've spread out from our native habitat in Africa to dominate every continent except Antarctica. The paleontologist and ecologist Richard Leakey noted, in the early 1990s, that "humans consume 40 percent of net primary productivity . . . on land; that is, the total energy trapped in photosynthesis worldwide, minus that required by the plants themselves for their survival." So, plant life all over the world captures more than enough energy from the sun to keep itself alive. All animal life depends on that surplus—and of that surplus, humans consume nearly half. Calculating a figure like that requires a lot of guesswork. But whatever number you come up with, it's certain that modern humans consume far more resources than any other species on the planet.

Exotic invasives have traveled with us through all the thousands of years we've traveled on Earth. The traffic of exotic invasives increased greatly during the heyday of European exploration and colonization of the world, from the sixteenth century to the late nineteenth century. Pigs, cattle, horses, sheep, rabbits, camels, and a host of diseases and parasites they carried were introduced to parts of the world where they'd never been before. In much of the Americas, Australia, and the Pacific Islands, these tagalong species either had no natural predators or were protected by humans. They so increased in numbers that native plants disappeared. Typically, the native plants that couldn't cope with the animal invaders were replaced by nonnative plants that had also tagged along with Europeans and their animals. These nonnative plants had coevolved with these animals and could better tolerate them.

SHIPBOARD ALIEN INVADERS

"Taken on to aid stability and propulsion, ballast water does for the modern cargo ship what sandbags do for a hot-air balloon. Unfortunately, it can also carry comb jellies from the East Coast to the Black Sea, Japanese sea stars to Australia, and voracious green crabs from Europe to San Francisco Bay.

"Many, perhaps most, of the organisms do not survive their odysseys. But with so much ballast water in motion around the world, many organisms inevitably do. And even one can inflict profound changes on its new habitat. The Eurasian zebra mussel reached Lake St. Clair via ballast water in the 1980s; it now lives throughout the Great Lakes, down the Mississippi River to New Orleans, and in more than 350 lakes and ponds. No larger than a pistachio, it thrives in such dense profusion that it has sunk navigational buoys. It crowds out native species and hogs the nutrients that other organisms require."

—*Alan Burdick*, Out of Eden: An Odyssey of Ecological Invasion, *2005*

Species such as ring-necked pheasant, feral pigs, and starlings that we consider wild in North America were introduced here intentionally from Europe or Asia. Starlings were brought to the United States in the 1890s by a man who thought that every songbird mentioned in William Shakespeare's writing should live in New York. They have spread to establish themselves in huge numbers across the continent. They outcompete such natives as bluebirds and flickers for food and other resources. The numbers of these native birds have decreased dramatically. Also introduced from Europe and Asia were a great many species we consider pests. These pests include parasites, weeds, fish that overwhelm waterways, and rats that plague cities. Quite a few people once thought it was a good idea to plant kudzu, a wildly invasive vine from Asia, for controlling erosion in the southeastern part of the United States.

The traffic of exotic invasives has further increased in recent years with the globalization of the world's economy. More and more products travel great distances to market. Too often, exotic invasive species tag along. Beetles come in wooden shipping crates, crabs are sucked in with ballast water into the holds of boats, and diseases are carried on ornamental plants.

Kudzu vines encase an old ruins in Rockingham, North Carolina. Kudzu plants grow rapidly, extending as much as 60 feet (18 m) per season at a rate of about 12 inches (30 cm) per day.

INVADED ISLANDS

Isolated islands are especially vulnerable to ill effects from exotic invasives. Their native species have evolved in contact with only the limited number of species present with them on their island. Therefore, they have no defenses against whole categories of predators and diseases not naturally found there. The Pacific island of Guam, for example, has lost most of its native bird species. They've been eaten by the nonnative, egg-eating brown tree snake since it was accidentally brought there half a century ago.

Habitat alteration can worsen the ill effects of exotic invaders. Many invasive species most easily establish themselves in disturbed habitat. (Kudzu and European pasture weeds such as dandelions are good examples of this.) Intact, naturally evolved ecological communities tend to have the most species diversity their setting can naturally support. This gives them a no-room-at-the-inn defense against exotic invaders. Disrupting the community by cutting trees or plowing native grasses weakens its defenses.

On the islands of Hawaii, for example, you can still find highland forests that have been little changed by human activities. These highland forest communities have been there a long time. They are mature, persistent, and hold all the species an ecologist would hope to find there. Nearby lowland forests have been altered by logging, road building, farming, and construction projects. In some places, these forests have been left alone long enough to recover their original number of species. But even there, they're relatively immature ecosystems. They're not as resistant to invaders as the undisturbed highland forests.

ISOLATED LAKES ARE LIKE ISLANDS

"In an aquatic mirror of terrestrial islands, isolated freshwater lakes and river ecosystems are very susceptible to invasive species. Introductions of non-native, often predatory fish can unravel diverse native fish assemblages in just a few years, precipitating a cascade of local extinctions. . . . None have been more devastated than the native cichlids [small fish that protect their young by carrying them in their mouths] of East Africa's Lake Victoria, the world's second-largest freshwater lake. The cichlid community was extraordinarily diverse, with over 300 specialized species, 99 percent of which occurred only in this lake. Unfortunately the community began to collapse during the 1980s following a population explosion of the Nile perch, a non-native predatory fish introduced to boost the lake fisheries. It did its job all too well, feeding indiscriminately on the much smaller cichlids and destroying native food webs."

— *John Tuxill*, Losing Strands in the Web of Life, *1998*

Cichlids are native to Lake Victoria and surrounding lakes in Uganda, Tanzania, and Kenya. Most of lakes' cichlids have become extinct.

Human newcomers have migrated to Hawaii again and again since the first Polynesians arrived there perhaps fifteen hundred years ago. Each wave of newcomers has brought alien plants and animals. Most of these alien invaders have arrived in the past two centuries. Each time an alien species has established itself, it has reduced the numbers of competing native species. Or it has set off a chain reaction of native extinctions. The alien species have mostly established themselves in the immature lowland forests. Fewer alien species have survived in the more mature highland ecosystems, which are more persistent, resilient, and resistant to invaders.

Some native species have migrated from disturbed lowland habitat to more intact highland forests. The shy po'ouli bird,

The po'ouli bird of Hawaii has vanished due to habitat destruction.

first discovered in 1974, was apparently one such refugee. But the shrinking highland refuges are not able to support the same populations of native species that they once could. Many of those reduced populations are as vulnerable to extinction as the North Atlantic right whales. Most species of native birds found only in Hawaii have become extinct or threatened. The last po'ouli bird died in captivity in November 2004.

FRAGMENTATION

The trail to Grinnell Glacier climbs and climbs, heading toward the Continental Divide in northwestern Montana. It goes past and often through many little streams fed by snowmelt. The trees grow smaller in the harsher, colder conditions here than they do farther down the mountain. The plant life here is adapted to a short growing season and more exposure to sun and wind.

Snowbanks on both sides of a stream indicate that ice bridged this stream just a few days ago. Although it's early July, winter is just ending here. Beyond that stream, the forest thins out into patches of stunted firs and shrubs. Rock dominates the landscape. Among the rocks, treeless gardens of subalpine and alpine wildflowers flourish, dazzling in their diversity, beautiful almost beyond belief. Along the side of the trail, grizzly bears looking for good roots to eat have torn up several patches of glacier lilies.

The grizzly bears and other animals that live here, along with the wild diversity of plant life, tell us that nearly the full array of species that could live here do so. It's an exceptionally large array. This is because here in the mountains of northern Montana, several habitat regions—Pacific Northwest, Canadian Rockies, and central Rockies—intersect.

Wildflowers and stunted trees grow along the Grinnell Glacier Trail in Glacier National Park in Montana.

But not far from here, human activities, from ranching to mining to road building to urban sprawl, have bit by bit isolated this wealth of wildlife. The wildlife here can no longer mingle and mate with others of their kind in a range large enough to ensure long-term survival. This habitat has effectively become an island.

The places where grizzly bears and other big predators are still found are reservoirs of life. They are refuges for healthy natural systems and genetic diversity. They are our last few remaining links to the wealth of life that thrived throughout North America three centuries ago. But most of these reservoirs of life are becoming or have already become too small, confined, isolated, and fragmented. From Maine to Appalachia to Montana to California, all U.S. forests are impaired by fragmentation. Fragmentation means that even where forest remains more or less undisturbed, it's cut off from other forest habitat by farmland and development. Fragmentation and habitat reduction are also affecting the United States' prairies and wetlands.

INLAND ISLANDS

Fragments of habitat hemmed in by farmland or pavement are effectively islands. Generally, the smaller the island, the smaller the number of species it can sustain. Biologists Edward O. Wilson and Robert MacArthur offer a rule of thumb. If Island A is ten times bigger than Island B and both have the same kind of habitat, Island A will support twice as many species. As a large expanse of habitat shrinks to a much smaller island, the number of species it supports shrinks too. This happens in several ways.

First, any species that requires a range larger than the remaining island of habitat will soon become locally extinct. A cougar that feeds on deer can't live in a patch too small to support enough deer to feed it.

Second, species that depend on the cougar or on other species too large for the shrunken habitat soon become extinct also. Studies in Brazil, for example, have looked at islands of habitat that have become too small to support peccaries. (The peccary is a native wild pig.) In these places, certain species of frogs will become extinct as well. The frogs depend on the peccaries' wallowing in dirt to make holes that fill with rain to become the ponds they need to live in.

Third and most important, the stresses that cause extinction have bigger effects in small islands of habitat. Small islands support only small populations. Small populations are more vulnerable to extinction. If something kills one hundred individuals out of a population of one thousand, then that population may recover. If one hundred individuals die where the total local population is only one hundred, then that species becomes locally extinct.

Fragmentation thus imitates and can also worsen the lingering aftereffects of hunting a species down to small numbers. In Asia, for example, tigers have been hunted so much that only a few thousand individuals remain. Fragmentation and habitat reduction have left these individuals separated into several even smaller groups. These groups are isolated from one another in scattered fragments of their former range. The groups are too small to be safe from the bad effects of inbreeding on their gene pool. The fragments of territory each group occupies are too small to allow a group to survive a local catastrophe. Their risk of extinction is high.

The pelt of a tiger—an endangered species—is for sale at this shop in Tachilek, Myanmar (formerly known as Burma).

BIG PREDATORS NEED BIG RANGES

Wolves and cougars once ranged all across the continental United States. Grizzly bears once ranged from the Pacific Ocean to the Mississippi River. In the twenty-first century, they're confined within much-reduced, unconnected fragments of their original ranges.

Plants and animals survive by spreading themselves over as wide a range as possible, which ensures that a local catastrophe such as fire can't destroy them all. They develop and maintain the genetic robustness, resilience, and diversity that enable

*Grizzly bears used to roam the entire western half of North America.
As the pioneers took over and farmed bear territory in the Midwest
and in the West in the 1800s, the bears vanished from much of their
former range. The bears can be found in Alaska, Wyoming, Montana,
Idaho, Washington, and a few western Canadian provinces.*

them to thrive by spreading their offspring over far-flung and
varied terrain. In these varied places, individual plants or animals with small genetic differences from others of their kind are
able to settle into bits of habitat for which they're especially
well suited and thrive there. When confined to a small fragment of habitat, even if wildlife survives, its genetic diversity
tends to diminish rather than increase.

As grizzly bears, for example, have retreated to a tiny fraction
of their former range, the largest, most wide-ranging, and most
fearless among them have been mostly killed by human

hunters. This means the surviving bears are smaller and shyer. They carry only a subset of their ancestors' genes. And they're cut off from breeding with others of their kind beyond the confines of their inland island. So, these bears will continue to diminish in both numbers and genetic robustness.

Even if we try to reintroduce big predators to places where they used to be, fragmentation threatens those efforts. Big predators need big ranges. Few habitats in the modern world offer enough room to keep the predators separate from humans and livestock. When a wolf roams into a human-occupied area, it's likely to be killed.

 ## THE EDGE EFFECT

The mirror image of wolves roaming outside their permitted island of habitat is the edge effect. This is the effect that stresses from outside the island have on the island habitat.

Stresses that can cause extinction surround each island of habitat. Their effects penetrate the habitat. At the edge of a forest, for example, plant life might be exposed to harsher winds. There is also more sunlight there, as well as slightly different weather and soil conditions. At the edge, alien invaders and human hunters enter the island and affect its ecology. Depending on local circumstances, edge effects can extend hundreds of feet or even miles in from the edge. Small islands thus may have no habitat that's beyond reach of the edge effect.

For example, North American songbirds living deep in a forest are not threatened by cowbirds. Cowbirds are native parasites. They lay their eggs in songbird nests to have their young raised by the songbirds. Cowbird chicks are big and aggressive. With a cowbird in the nest, the songbirds' own chicks

The larger cowbird chick is fed by a yellow warbler mother. As cowbirds lay eggs in other birds' nests, their young eat more of the food, causing the other chicks to die. Songbird populations are greatly affected in areas where cowbird ranges overlap their own.

die. Cowbirds feed in open fields and backyards, not in forests. On land fragmented by agriculture and development, with only small islands of forest remaining, cowbirds prevent songbirds from raising enough young to replace themselves. Only songbird nesting sites deep enough in the forest to be 4 miles (6.5 km) from the nearest cowbird feeding area are safe from cowbirds. In the twenty-first century, most islands of forest in the midwestern United States are too small to have any such sites. Only a few large patches of forest in the region (in the Ozark Mountains, mostly) support healthy songbird populations with growing numbers. Songbirds fly out from these few places and replace those killed by cowbirds elsewhere.

HEATH HENS

The heath hen is a sad example of a once-widespread and numerous species hunted to a tiny remnant and then confined to an island of habitat. This put it at very high risk for extinction. "Originally [the heath hen's] range stretched from Maine to Virginia, but by 1908 intensive hunting, combined with a loss of habitat through human population expansion, reduced the birds to only fifty individuals, isolated on the island of Martha's Vineyard, off the coast of Massachusetts. . . . A refuge of some sixteen-hundred acres [650 hectares] was established to protect the remaining birds and to boost their population. By 1915, the project was gaining momentum, with two thousand birds in the refuge. Then disaster struck, or rather a series of disasters. Fire, a hard winter, the inimical effects of inbreeding, and a poultry disease reduced the population to a mere eleven males and two females in 1927. The last bird was seen on 11 March 1932."

—*Richard Leakey and Roger Lewin,* The Sixth Extinction, *1995*

This heath hen is on display at the Field Museum in Chicago, Illinois.

If it weren't for this flow of replacement songbirds from the few remaining large forests in the region, the Midwest's smaller islands of forest would have no songbirds left at all. If those few remaining larger patches of forest disappear or become fragmented, songbirds will likely become extinct throughout the entire region.

THEY NEED HABITAT, AND THEIR HABITAT NEEDS THEM

The fragments of habitat where big predators still live are poor remnants of their former ranges. At the same time, the places where they no longer roam are made poorer by their absence. The loss of a habitat's top predator sets off a cascade of disruptions to the web of life there. This is because all large animals—and top predators especially—have large impacts on their habitats. They curb the population of animals they prey upon. They eat and disperse seeds. They create distinctive minihabitats where they wallow, root, or bed down. Other animals, plants, and parasites depend on these impacts. When a large animal becomes locally or globally extinct, the others may too.

Even small animals have important effects on their habitats. When fragmentation threatens forest-dwelling birds, for example, it also threatens the trees that shelter them.

The same songbirds that are threatened by cowbirds in the Midwest eat a lot of insects. Researchers have tried fencing birds out of oak forest there with netting, to see what happens. What happens is that caterpillars eat much more of the trees' leaves. The trees grow much more slowly there than in a forest with a normal population of birds.

Chapter 7

CLIMATE CHANGE

Grinnell Glacier and the other glaciers of Montana have been shrinking since the last ice age. In recent years, they've been melting faster and faster. This is because the whole world's climate is warming. The twenty-first century has already seen the warmest year since reliable temperature records began to be kept in the 1890s. As of the end of 2006, the ten warmest years on record had occured within the last twelve years. Scientists expect this warming trend to continue. Most scientists agree that we humans are causing or at least greatly adding to global warming. Because of this warming, all Montana's glaciers may be gone within the next quarter century. At the same time, global climate change is expected to have great effects on patterns of plant and animal life. It also affects species extinction.

The Continental Divide forms the higher side of the bowl of rock that holds Grinnell Glacier. Patches of stunted firs mingle with patches of wildflower garden and patches of bare rock all the way up to the wall of steep bare rock at the top of the Great Divide. There's just barely room for the alpine wildflower gardens between the subalpine forest below and the wall of rock above.

Given just a slight warming shift in climate, trees may find more places where they can live higher up the mountain. Bit by bit, this place could come to look the way nearby mountaintops at slightly lower elevation look. There would be a lake where

Grinnell Lake in Glacier National Park (facing page) *looks milky because of the tiny particles of rock suspended in the runoff from the glacier.*

Grinnell Glacier sits. The lake would be surrounded by thick subalpine forest blanketing the mountains all the way up to near-vertical bare rock. There would be no more alpine wildflower gardens. A world in which Montana loses all its high-country wildflower gardens would be sadly diminished, even if it gained more beautiful subalpine lakes.

This is a best-case scenario. More likely, global warming will hit this fragile landscape with changes faster and bigger than it can withstand. Greater summer heat on the bare rock might kill off the alpine wildflowers before shrubs and trees can take root in the scanty soil the flowers hold in place. What if the snowfields here melt earlier each year? Their slow trickle down the mountainside might then end in June rather than July. This would start the summer dry season a month early. What if changes in the weather stress certain trees or shrubs while helping their pests? The trees or shrubs could die in great numbers. (This is already happening with beetle-infested pine forests throughout the West.) What will happen to the marmots (large ground squirrels) and ptarmigans (chickenlike birds) if tree line and ice disappear and their mountaintops become engulfed in forest? Marmots and ptarmigans are well adapted for life amid the rocks and ice at tree line. They don't live in forests. And what will happen to the grizzly bears? We've already reduced their range to fragments. Warmer weather is already enabling beetles to destroy the whitebark pines whose seeds the bears formerly relied upon. The roots of glacier lilies are favored foods for bears in early spring. What will happen to the bears if the glacier lilies disappear with their alpine habitat?

Long-term temperature changes also are a natural part of the way the world works. Ice ages alternate with warm spells. If the changes come about slowly enough, many species can either adapt to the new weather or migrate to more appropriate climates. But what if change is faster, taking decades rather than hundreds or even thousands of years? This could cause a catastrophic mass extinction of species.

Is that happening? The hugely complex research on this question is far from complete. Still, many scientists believe that human activities are driving such a sudden global climate change.

 GREENHOUSE EFFECT

Global warming comes about through what we call the greenhouse effect. This effect is caused by certain gases in the atmosphere. These include carbon dioxide, methane, water vapor, and others. These gases act like the glass in a greenhouse or the closed windows of a car. They allow the sun's warmth to reach Earth while preventing much of that captured warmth from radiating back out into space. Without this natural greenhouse effect,

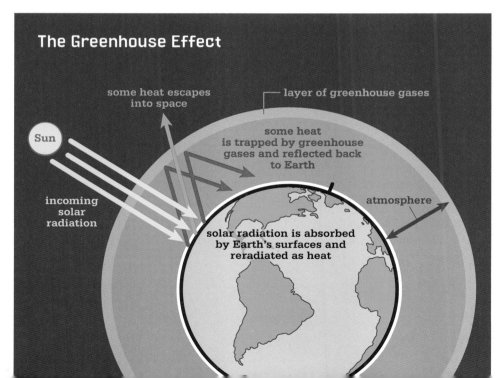

The Greenhouse Effect

the average temperature on Earth would be well below freezing. Life as we know it could not have evolved here.

Over the past century or so, humans have pumped huge amounts of greenhouse gases into the atmosphere. This change is very sudden, as such global events go. We have doubled the amount of methane. We have increased the carbon dioxide in the atmosphere from 290 to 370 parts per million by volume. Most of that increase has come in the past half century. As recently as 1945, the carbon dioxide level was just 300 parts per million.

We have made this change in two ways. First, we've burned huge amounts of fuel derived from plants. These fuels include wood, charcoal, coal, oil, and natural gas. In doing this, we have suddenly, in only a few centuries, released the carbon taken out of the atmosphere and stored by plant life over millions of years. Second, in cutting the world's forests, we have stopped their natural removal of carbon from the air. We have also turned former forestland to other uses such as factories, livestock farms, or rice paddies. These uses generate still more greenhouse gases.

Earth's climate is very complex. Our understanding of how many factors work together to influence it is primitive. Even our best computer models can't say precisely what effect the greenhouse gases we've added to the air are having or will have on the world's climate.

Waiting until science sorts all this out is risky. The risk is waiting until it's too late to avoid mass species extinctions. It may be too late already. Even if we completely stopped adding more greenhouse gases to the air tomorrow, the effects of what we've already done would continue to stoke global warming for the next century.

POTENTIAL FOR DISASTER

Global warming is a systemic alteration to the natural order. That human activities are at least part of the cause for this is without precedent. Humans have never done such a thing to global ecology before. Global warming changes the way nature works, everywhere. It does this in unpredictable ways that make our planet less productive and hospitable for us. The effects and costs of this change are beyond our ability to fully understand.

We've all heard warnings about potential effects of global warming that sound like scenes from a horror movie. For example, melting polar icecaps would cause the sea level to rise and wash away coastal cities around the world. Some climate models say that global warming fueled by human activities could cause the planet's climate to "flip" from hot to cold. If

THE END OF NATURE

"Our comforting sense of the permanence of our natural world, our confidence that it will change gradually and imperceptibly if at all, is . . . the result of a subtly warped perspective. Changes that can affect us can happen in our lifetime in our world—not just changes like wars but bigger and more sweeping events. I believe that without recognizing it we have already stepped over the threshold of such a change: that we are at the end of nature. . . . We have changed the atmosphere, and that will change the weather. The temperature and rainfall are no longer to be entirely the work of some separate, uncivilizable force, but instead in part a product of our habits, our economies, our ways of life."

—*Bill McKibben*, The End of Nature, *1989*

that happened, Earth could be sent into a deep freeze that would extinguish most life.

We don't know how extreme the effects of global warming will be. But we can expect those effects to include changes in the timing of seasons. We'll likely see changes in rainfall, with some places wetter and some drier. We'll also likely see changes in ocean currents. And we can expect to see more extreme weather, such as droughts, hurricanes, and tornadoes. There's evidence that all of these changes have already begun.

Each of these changes can be expected to cause at least local extinction for some species. For example, polar bears will likely become extinct in Alaska within the next century. This will hap-

A satellite photograph shows Hurricane Katrina bearing down on the southern coast of the United States in August 2005. The hurricane caused incredible damage to coastal areas of Louisiana and Mississippi. Global warming and climate change will likely result in a higher number of such extreme storms.

WILL WE CHANGE OUR MINDS?

"What kind of issue is like this that we've faced in the past? . . . I think it's the kind of issue where something looked extremely difficult, and not worth it, and then people changed their minds. . . . Slavery . . . had some of those characteristics 150 years ago. Some people thought it was wrong, and they made their arguments, and they didn't carry the day. And then something happened and all of a sudden it was wrong and we didn't do it anymore. And there were social costs to that. I suppose cotton was more expensive. We said, 'That's the trade-off; we don't want to do this anymore.' So we may look at [global warming] and say, 'We are tampering with the earth.' The earth is a twitchy system. It's clear from the record that it does things that we don't fully understand. And we're not going to understand them in the time period we have to make these decisions. . . . We may say, 'We just don't want to do this to ourselves.' If it's a problem like that, then asking whether it's practical or not is really not going to help very much. Whether it's practical depends on how much we give a damn."

—physicist Robert Socolow, quoted by Elizabeth Kolbert in "The Climate of Man" (The New Yorker), 2005

pen as warming melts the state's few remaining fragments of the icy habitat the bears require. Altogether, these changes will likely trigger a cascade of global extinctions of many species.

Global warming worsens the effects of all the other human activities that push species toward extinction. (It also can actually worsen itself. As Arctic tundra melts and the soils of temperate zones warm, natural processes of decay in those soils speed up. The decay generates carbon dioxide. This process further stokes global warming. The warmer climate warms the soil further and so on.) Species already stressed and reduced in number from being hunted too much, from exotic invaders, or from reduced or fragmented habitat are especially at risk for extinction as the climate changes. Their reduced numbers or reduced ranges make it less likely they'll be able to move to other places as climate change makes their current habitat unlivable for them.

CHANGES WE ALREADY SEE

The timing of the famous cherry blossom season in Washington, D.C., varies a good bit from year to year. But overall, by the beginning of the twenty-first century, on average, the trees were blooming about a week earlier than they were just three decades earlier. Farther north, in central Massachusetts, spring begins with maple sugaring. Maple trees are tapped for their sweet sap when daytime temperatures climb above freezing but

Tourists enjoy the blossoming cherry trees near the Jefferson Memorial in Washington, D.C. Global warming has caused the trees to bloom earlier than they had just thirty years ago.

frost still forms at night, causing the maple trees' sap to rise. These days, this usually occurs in February. In the mid-nineteenth century, it came a week or two later, in March. These and other details tell us that the entire Northern Hemisphere's spring is coming more than a week earlier than it used to. This is one sign of global warming.

Global warming and related climate change have already created many other effects we can see and measure. Grizzly bears have moved far north of their normal range. They're way up into the Canadian Arctic, eating food that local polar bears rely on. Ocean currents have shifted. Birds and land animals have changed their migration patterns. Blooming times of plants and breeding habits of animals have changed. Whole populations of certain migrating birds have shifted their breeding grounds north.

HORSESHOE CRABS AND RED KNOTS, WARBLERS AND CATERPILLARS

South of Wilmington, Delaware, on the sandy beaches of the Delaware Bay, horseshoe crabs the size and shape of shallow helmets head toward shore to spawn each spring. This ancient species lives from Maine to Mexico. But the bay here is the strong center of their population. Millions of them breed along the Delaware Bay. They crawl up out of the water on nights when the tide is high and the surf is gentle. Then they fertilize and deposit billions of soft greenish eggs in the sand. Horseshoe crabs spawn from April to August. By far most of them come ashore during evening full-moon high tides in May and June. The peak is around the full moon in mid-May. Two weeks later, on the lesser but still quite high new-moon tide, the hatchlings will crawl up out of the sand to be washed out to sea.

A mass of horseshoe crabs climbs up the sandy beaches in Delaware Bay. Ruddy turnstones (above) *and red knots, common shorebirds, feed on the horseshoe crab's eggs. If the horseshoe crab's egg-laying period is altered due to an early arrival of warmer weather, migrating shorebirds that rely on the eggs for their long journey may disappear.*

Delaware Bay is also a crucial stopping point for perhaps a million or more of several species of shorebirds migrating from South America to the far north. They land there to feed on the crab eggs. They used to feed elsewhere as well. But most of the once-vast Atlantic tidal marshland has been lost to development and erosion. So these birds depend on the rich and abundant crab eggs of Delaware Bay to fuel their long flight. The Americas' entire population of red knots, a robin-sized sandpiper, flies north from the southern tip of South America. They stop here briefly to feed on the crab eggs. Then they fly on to nest on islands as much as 1,000 miles (1,610 km) farther north, in the Canadian Arctic. It's hard to imagine a more wide-ranging example of nature's connectedness than this.

Jennifer Ackerman, a writer, has closely observed horseshoe crab spawning on one of the bay's beaches. She explains how global warming may be uncoupling this matchup of predator and prey. "If the earth warms, chances are that the two critical timing signals . . . —length of day and temperature—will uncouple," she writes. "Day length, the signal that gets a shorebird up and out of Patagonia one evening in March, won't change, but temperatures will." If the ocean warms earlier in the year, horseshoe crabs will be cued to lay their eggs earlier. "So a migrating bird that arrives at its northern feeding and breeding grounds on schedule will miss the emergence of its prey. I wonder what will happen to red knots if the horseshoe crabs of Delaware Bay spawn in April instead of May."

Most likely, they'll die. Perhaps the greatest effect of global warming won't be melting glaciers or rising sea level but the uncoupling of countless such natural matches. Food, water, shelter, or hiding places for young may no longer be there when needed.

Inland a little ways from the Delaware Bay, a similar story plays out. A great wave of dozens of species of the little migrating birds called warblers rolls up from the south each spring. The warbler wave closely follows the appearance of new leaves on hardwood trees. These trees dominate the inland forests of eastern North America. As the trees' tender new leaves emerge, inchworms and other such chewing insects emerge to eat the leaves. These insects, in turn, are eaten by the warblers. At the peak of the warbler migration, an experienced bird-watcher might see a dozen different species of

American warblers spend their winters in Central and South America. In the spring, they migrate to the United States and Canada. Their journeys may involve nonstop flights covering more than a thousand miles (kilometers) at a time. When they finally touch down, they must feed constantly to refuel. If the insects warblers rely on during their migration are not available, the birds' survival may be in jeopardy.

warblers in a single early-morning hour, plus many other song-birds, woodpeckers, and more.

Most of the warblers come from the tropics. Like the shore-birds that land at Delaware Bay, they are cued to begin migra-tion each spring by changes in day length. What will happen to the warblers if the insects they expect to find up here hatch ear-lier, cued by warmer climate? If they hatch earlier, they could mature from the soft, sweet crawling things the birds eat into winged forms before the birds arrive. What will happen to the trees if warblers aren't there in time to eat the caterpillars?

Chapter 8

PERVASIVE POISONS

After World War II (1939–1945) came a huge increase in the industrialized world's production and use of synthetic chemicals. These include many different kinds of pesticides. In 1962 the book *Silent Spring*, by biologist Rachel Carson, focused public attention on how the heavy use of chemicals by North American farmers was affecting wildlife—and humans. Many of these chemicals, Carson explained, persist for years in the environment. They build up higher and higher levels as farmers spread them on fields each year. Some of these chemicals concentrate as they make their way through the food web. Larger animals—including humans—accumulate higher concentrations of toxins than the smaller animals and plants they eat. This accumulation creates a potent risk for humans.

Carson's book touched off widespread public fears about the environmental and health effects of pollution from the products and by-products of modern industry. Pesticide use has been only one of many areas of concern about pollution. Others include air pollution, water pollution, tainted food, nuclear contamination, and how to dispose of garbage and hazardous wastes. Nor is the concern about pesticides and other industrial chemicals limited to "persistent" synthetics. (These are manufactured chemicals that remain intact and potent for long periods of time even when exposed to weather.) Fertilizer runoff from farmland, for example, has entered most U.S. waterways over the past half century. This is so even though the fertilizer chemicals break down fairly quickly.

That the air might not be safe to breathe was the first widespread public fear about pollution. Concern about the fallout from nuclear bomb testing led to the 1963 Nuclear Test Ban Treaty. This banned aboveground tests of nuclear weapons. Smog generated by cars concentrated in urban areas was first noticed in Los Angeles in the 1940s. It became visible in city after city in the years after *Silent Spring*. And the public began to be aware of the problem of acid rain caused by emissions from industrial smokestacks polluting the air. Acid rain can harm forests and lakes hundreds of miles downwind.

POISONING OURSELVES

"We have put poisonous and biologically potent chemicals indiscriminately into the hands of persons largely or wholly ignorant of their potentials for harm. We have subjected enormous numbers of people to contact with these poisons, without their consent and often without their knowledge. If the Bill of Rights contains no guarantee that a citizen shall be secure against lethal poisons distributed either by private individuals or by public officials, it is surely because our forefathers, despite their considerable wisdom and foresight, could conceive of no such problem."

—*Rachel Carson* (right),
Silent Spring, *1962*

CFCS AND THE OZONE LAYER

Global warming is not the only wide-ranging systemic alteration we've made to the way nature works. We've altered not only the temperature but also the content of the air. We have increased the amount of carbon dioxide. We've thinned the upper atmosphere's protective ozone layer. We've created large amounts of smoke that makes rain acidic. And many of the effects of global warming, ozone thinning, and acid rain are amplified when they're combined as has happened over the past decades.

In the twentieth century, engineers developed a class of chemicals known as chlorofluorocarbons (CFCs). Their unusual chemical stability made them useful in many kinds of industrial and consumer goods, such as aerosol sprays, refrigerators, and air conditioners. But their stability also has meant that, once released into the air, CFCs persist for decades. They slowly drift into the upper layers of the atmosphere. There, they participate in chemical reactions that consume ozone. (Ozone is a gas that in the upper atmosphere helps filter harmful ultraviolet radiation from the sun.)

As early as 1974, scientists thought that CFCs might be destroying the atmosphere's ozone layer. Losing all or much of the ozone layer would increase the likelihood of certain skin cancers. It would also pose unknown, possibly disastrous threats to the world's plant and animal life. By the 1980s, people around the world concluded that this problem was real. They agreed that the risks of allowing more and more CFCs to be released into the air outweighed even the huge economic benefits of continuing to use them.

In 1990 the United States and ninety-two other nations agreed to stop using CFCs altogether by the year 2000. As international agreements go, the world's response to the CFC-ozone problem was remarkably swift. (It took years rather than decades to agree on it.) It was also effective. Luckily, the chemical industry was able to develop substitutes for CFCs quickly. However, because CFCs linger so long in the air, it's not yet clear how much damage they will ultimately do. Also, we don't fully know how the increase in ultraviolet radiation caused by CFCs will interact with other, on-going human alterations to the environment.

FIDDLER CRABS AND FROGS

The effects of pervasive poisons, together with our other wide-ranging alterations to the biosphere, are many, varied, interactive, and often surprising. And for the most part, they are poorly understood.

For example, wetlands scientist Ken Scarlatelli can tell you about a study of fiddler crabs at northern New Jersey's Meadowlands. The Meadowlands is a swampy place that's long been a dumping ground for New York City. The crabs studied there didn't seem to be affected in any clear way by living in mud contaminated with mercury, a highly toxic heavy metal. Lots of bigger animals eat the crabs, though. Probably, those animals accumulate higher doses of mercury than the crabs do. But "exhaustive studies haven't been done" on those animals, Scarlatelli notes. Elsewhere, he says, scientists have tried to study birds that eat metal-contaminated prey. But the effects are subtle. "There's speculation that they may suffer impairment of their visual acuity," Scarlatelli says, "So it may make it harder for them to catch prey, so they may actually die of starvation. *Maybe.*" Most of the high-on-the-food-chain predators—herons, egrets, and double-crested cormorants—aren't in the

Fiddler crabs feed by sifting through the sands on which they live, thus aerating them. Some scientists believe this feeding habit plays a major role in the preservation of wetlands.

Meadowlands year-round. Perhaps spending winters or summers in cleaner places limits their total intake of toxins to levels they can tolerate. Maybe.

The question is how much poison, in how many places, is ultimately too much? How many species are we nudging toward extinction in ways we don't even understand?

Consider, for example, the decline of frogs. All over the world, even in places that seem quite unchanged by humans, the number of frogs is shrinking. Frog deformity and disease are increasing. We don't fully understand why this is happening. But that it is happening is beyond dispute. Scientists think that most of the frogs' problems come from factors that amplify one another. These factors include acid rain, ozone thinning, global warming, and likely others we haven't yet identified. Separately or together, these factors harm frogs directly or weaken their resistance to disease. (Frogs nearly everywhere have come to be afflicted by an exotic invasive fungus that

Malformed frogs, such as this seven-legged frog from Marin County, California, may be indicators that our environment is changing.

humans spread from Africa in the mid-twentieth century.) In many places where frog decline has been observed, synthetic chemicals in the water where frogs live seem to have played a role. For example, estrogens from human medicine flushed into surface water and the common farm herbicide atrazine are both thought to disrupt frogs' hormone functions.

Frogs are not the only creatures affected by chemicals in the water in which they live. River otters, turtles, birds, and fish also have been affected. In at least some places, scientists have found that synthetic estrogens and other chemicals in the water have disrupted animals' fertility.

Dozens of animal species, such as fish, bears, and eagles, have been found to accumulate various synthetic chemicals in their bodies. The effects of this accumulation are largely unknown. Rainfall, water runoff, and the food web have spread persistent synthetic chemicals virtually everywhere in the world. Often chemicals show up in surprising places and in unexpected amounts. Polar bears are contaminated with flame retardants and other industrial chemicals. Seawater teems with microscopic bits of plastic. Mercury from coal-burning power plants is found in fish in lakes all over the United States. The more carefully we look, the more such examples we see.

Chapter 9

TIPPING POINT?

Think of a cereal box sitting on a table. Push against one side of the box, near the top. The box will tip as you push it—until it reaches a certain point. Then it will suddenly and quickly fall. Is biodiversity on Earth approaching such a tipping point? Have the human activities that drive species to extinction pushed so far that we're on the brink of a fast fall into extinction of most of the planet's species? Anne and Paul Ehrlich's "rivet-popper" hypothesis asks much the same question. Have we popped so many rivets (extinguished so many species) that the whole airplane (the web of life on Earth) is about to come crashing down?

HOW LITTLE WE KNOW

We can't answer this question with any certainty. Our knowledge about things needed to answer it is too incomplete.

We don't even know how many species are sharing this planet with us. We have so far named only about 1.5 million living species. For some groups of species, our named list is probably nearly complete. Birds, mammals, and butterflies are large, attractive creatures that scientists like to study. So we know a good bit about them. For other groups (fungi and bacteria) our list of named species is no more than a small fraction of the total. We don't even know how big that fraction is. About two-thirds of the 1.5 million living species science knows about are from the world's temperate zones. This is because most of the world's scientists live there. But we know

 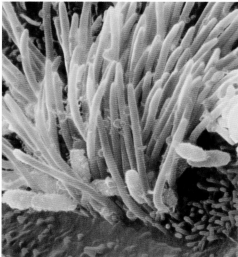

Scientists are working hard to discover and study the world's existing species before they disappear. Exciting species, such as the blue morpho butterfly (left), may attract more attention from non-scientists than microscopic bacteria, such as Bordetella pertussis (right, yellow green), which causes whooping cough. But as we're discovering, the impact of any one species loss may affect many others.

that the tropics hold far more species than temperate and arctic places. Our knowledge of marine species is also grossly incomplete. The most credible estimates of the total number of species currently living on Earth range from 10 million to 30 million. (Or from 5 million to 100 million, depending on how far you think "credible" stretches.)

Given this uncertainty, it makes sense that estimates of how many species are likely to be lost over the next century also vary a great deal. Estimating future species loss involves a lot of guesswork. First, there's the guess about how many species there are to begin with. Then you have to guess how much habitat is going to change in the future. How severe will the changes be? Where and how species rich will the most affected habitats be? How big or small will the fragments of habitat that remain be? And what will be the effects of other stresses, such as global warming and pollution?

Most of the experts who have looked closely at these questions have concluded that current extinctions are well above the background extinction rate. Typical estimates say that they exceed the background rate thousands of times over. These experts generally agree that the rate of extinctions is increasing significantly. Less agreement exists on exactly how rapidly extinctions are increasing. Altogether, these estimates tell us that if current trends continue, one-quarter to one-half of the world's species that lived in the late twentieth century are expected to become extinct within this century. Perhaps two-thirds or more will be extinct soon after.

RED LIST

One thing we do know is that thousands of the species science has named are currently threatened with extinction. The World Conservation Union has on its carefully compiled 2006 Red List 16,118 species known to be threatened with extinction. This number is up from 15,503 in 2004. These numbers are surely low. The Red List includes only species scientists know well enough to see they are in danger.

The Red List numbers look especially grim when you compare threatened species with the total number of known species in their classes. The Red List tells us that 20 percent of known mammals and 12 percent of known birds are threatened with extinction. Nearly half of the world's primates, the animals with genes most like our own, are threatened. Worse yet, this is just the tip of the iceberg. We know that many species of large, visible animals and plants are in danger of extinction.

Smaller, less visible species are threatened too. We know this in part because we know their ecosystems are being harmed by the changes described in this book. But we also know this because if the Red Listed species die, so will about seventy-five hundred more species that scientists know depend on them. In addition, an unknown but surely large number of species we don't know about or haven't looked at closely are at risk.

LIVING DEAD

A good many threatened species could be considered "living dead." Their numbers have already been very much reduced. They will almost certainly soon be done in by further stresses caused by humans or by natural stress episodes (fire, drought, and epidemic) that a larger, stronger population could survive. The North Atlantic right whales are probably "living dead." The few hundred that survived into the twenty-first century are likely the last of their kind. Scientists knew that Hawaii's po'ouli bird was doomed well before the last one died.

In the early 1990s, 135 native bird species were known to still be living in Hawaii. One scientist noted that fewer than a dozen of these species were doing well enough so that scientists were confident they would continue to survive. Another dozen species (including the po'ouli bird) were in such trouble that they were almost certainly doomed. Yet another dozen were listed as endangered. At the time, there was hope that these birds might be saved from extinction. In the years since then, that hope has faded. In 2004 the American Bird Conservancy noted that most of Hawaii's remaining native bird species were headed for extinction.

Even species that entered the twenty-first century with pretty good numbers might be among the living dead. Some, we know, are poised on the brink of a population crash that could wipe them out within a human lifetime. Sage grouses, for example, live in drier parts of the North American West. They've seen their range shrink to a fragmented fraction of what it used to be, due to farming and development. Their population is stable for the moment. But they could be at their tipping point. Their habitat continues to be consumed by development and invasive cheatgrass. Their numbers could crash suddenly.

The male sage grouse during a courtship display. This species may be on its way to extinction.

The world's species are dying out at an alarming rate. Above are just a handful of species and their status on the endangered species list (left to right from top): Santa Catalina Island rattlesnake (critically endangered), western lowland gorilla (critically endangered), Yangtze River dolphin (critically endangered, may be extinct), Egyptian vulture (endangered), humphead parrotfish (vulnerable).

Also among the living dead are species about to be extinguished before we even know about them. In 1978 scientists first visited a ridge called Centinela, in Ecuador, South America. There they found ninety unknown species of plants that lived nowhere else. Eight years later, the ridge had become farmland. All of its endemic species were extinct. Ecologists call such events centinelan extinctions. Surely similar events continue to happen in unique habitats unknown to science.

IGNORANCE OF HOW ECOSYSTEMS WORK

As we have seen, each individual species extinction sets off a cascade of changes. Some species that directly depend on the newly extinct species soon become extinct as well. Others experience new stresses that may push them toward extinction too. These stresses affect most or all of the species in the newly extinct species' ecosystem. We don't know nearly enough to say exactly what the full effects of any particular extinction on the rest of its ecosystem will be. Species that seem "useless" to us can be essential to their local web of life. Nor do we know the full story of how those effects will interact with stresses from human activities. We do know that those interactions make further extinctions more likely, possibly pushing that ecosystem beyond its tipping point. And what we do know ought to make us want to be more cautious than we've been about altering our ecological life-support system.

For example, the forests of New England in recent years have seen widespread declines of trees not usually considered at risk for any of the known exotic disease invaders. We don't fully understand why butternut, white ash, red oak, and sugar maple trees are declining. But they appear to be stressed and therefore more vulnerable to disease. Since the decline is widespread, it's a good guess that it's related to widespread environmental changes that we know have been taking place at the same time. These changes include acid rain, global warming, and increased ultraviolet light due to thinning of the ozone layer. Fragmentation of forests by human development is another such change. We know that fragmentation affects animal life in forests, though we don't fully understand how. Its effects on plant life, so closely involved with animals, are even less understood.

Meanwhile, changes in tropical forests are literally making us sick. Logging, road building, and other habitat changes, as well as climate change, all have changed these forests greatly. Diseases previously not seen in humans have been able to make new contacts with us in the altered ecosystems, in places or circumstances humans have rarely seen in the past. Some diseases have jumped to us from other animal species, as HIV (human immunodeficiency virus) is believed to have jumped to human hunters butchering wild animals. We're also seeing more of certain diseases favored by changed conditions (such as warmer climate) and old diseases appearing in places they've not been seen before. If we humans are suffering from this situation, likely, other species are as well. This places yet another set of stresses on already-stressed species. We've barely begun to assess the effects.

Even if we knew much, much more than we do about how Earth's many ecosystems work, we still could not predict for sure that any of the stresses we're creating are safe for any particular system. Consider the ocean. Anyone who fishes will tell you that fish populations sometimes rise or fall in ways that can't be predicted. Surprisingly big changes in fish population are apparently natural, driven by the inner workings of the ecosystem. Scientists confirm that there's an unavoidable element of chaos in natural systems, not a predictably stable balance of nature. This chaos can encourage biodiversity. A stable ecosystem can settle down into domination by one or just a few species. But the unsettling effects of wide swings in population can make room for more species. Dealing with unpredictable, unsettled ecosystems makes it harder for us to know the full effects of any changes we humans introduce. In fact, mathematical models suggest that it's impossible.

Northern fur seals, with pups, are dying out in Alaska.

Scientists see declines in many species for no clear reason. For example, northern fur seals recovered nicely a century ago after their mass slaughter for the fur trade ended. But they are dying out in Alaska. They've lost half their population there in the past half century. Their decline in numbers is accelerating after a stable period in the mid-1980s and 1990s. The scientists who study them don't know why. Hunting of the seals is minimal. Neither entanglement with fishing gear nor changes in their food supply nor increases in the number of killer whales that eat them seem enough to explain such a sharp decline.

"The marine system is a rich, complex field that has lots of influences," whale expert Stormy Mayo explains. "There are obviously yet-undescribed high levels of things [that] have basic, very profound effects." We not only don't understand what these effects are, "we don't even look at 'em. We don't know all of this stuff. We have these bare scribbles, and the scribbles are almost unintelligible translations of what really goes on."

Conclusion

WHAT NEXT?

Over the next fifty years, the number of humans on Earth is expected to grow from more than six billion to nine billion. Most of that growth will come in the most biodiverse, least industrialized parts of the world. As people living there seek the living standards of the world's more industrial nations, human consumption of natural resources is projected to grow even faster than human population. If past history is any guide, with growing numbers and more industry, all the human effects that increase species extinction will grow as well. We will see more habitat alteration and fragmentation. There will be more hunting and fishing, invasions by exotic species, climate change, and pervasive poisons. If we've not already gone past the tipping point toward mass extinction, it appears that we may be well along the path to doing so.

However, humans are the cleverest species ever to live on this planet. Our knowledge of science and understanding of nature is still very incomplete. But it's greater than it's ever been before. We could, if we choose to do so, apply that knowledge to sustaining Earth's current level of biodiversity. We could work with nature to find ways of supporting ourselves that don't further damage the biosphere.

There are plenty of purely selfish reasons why people should be concerned about the world's loss of biodiversity. Earth's life-forms depend on one another for survival in ways that are sometimes obvious and sometimes not. It makes sense to wonder how many holes can be eaten away from this web of life (or how many rivets can pop) before it will no longer support the human species.

Lost species can be an economic loss as well. When a species dies, its genes die with it. Modern science is only beginning to understand the ways in which Earth's gene resources might be useful to us. In addition to the loss of life involved, each species extinction might be taking economically valuable resources forever out of our reach. This almost happened with the rosy periwinkle, a plant from which potent cancer-fighting drugs have been derived. Luckily for us, this use for the plant was discovered before its entire habitat was destroyed. (It grew only in tropical forests in Madagascar. Most of those forests have been cut down.)

Economic losses from human actions that reduce biodiversity are much broader than this. Nature provides a host of services that have real economic value. For example, natural systems provide food and clean water. They control floods and create soil. Recently, more than thirteen hundred researchers from ninety-five countries made a survey of such "ecosystem services." They concluded that nearly two-thirds of those services are currently being degraded or reduced, directly or indirectly, by human actions.

Biodiversity isn't spread evenly over the planet. Tropical places tend to have more species than places with cooler climates. Habitat changed by such human activities as farming and tree cutting tend to have fewer species. So much of the world's remaining stock of gene resources is concentrated in less-developed parts of the world.

The mostly impoverished people who live among these resources are more likely to conserve them if it pays off for them. They're less likely to do so if the only profit is for the companies who develop those resources into marketable goods. Profit for local people might be in jobs or money to run conservation programs. Or they might share in genetic property rights, getting a share of the money earned from products derived from local plants or animals.

The biosphere is the huge but finite community of all living beings and the environment that sustains them. It is the super-community in which all our human communities are embedded. Obviously, all of us depend on it for life itself. But this is a deeply radical idea in the modern industrialized world. Accepting that the biosphere is our community makes it obvious that nature isn't something we go visit "out there." Nor is it something we can use however we wish without serious risk. For us, as for every species on Earth, it's our life-support system, the only one we've got.

GLOSSARY

background extinction rate: the normal rate at which species go extinct under relatively stable environmental conditions

biodiversity: short for "biological diversity," the term refers to the presence of many different species

biosphere: the layer of soil, water, and air in which all life on Earth takes place

canopy: the top-most level of a forest

edge effect: effects on habitat bordering a very different kind of habitat

endemic species: a species found naturally only in one home region

evolution: the theory developed by Charles Darwin in the mid-1800s that all new species arise as a result of natural selection of small variations that improve individuals' fitness for survival and reproduction

exotic invasive: a species that doesn't occur naturally in a certain place but, having been brought there by humans, does so well that it overwhelms native species

extinction: death of a species, after which no more of its kind exist

extinction crisis: a time of great environmental change when many or most of the species then living go extinct

food web: a network of species that eat and are eaten by one another; also called a food chain

fragmentation: the cutting of habitat into smaller, disconnected pieces separated by lands altered for human uses

genes: structures found in every cell that encode all the biological information an individual is born with

greenhouse effect: warming caused when sunlight passes through glass or when atmospheric gases let in solar energy more easily than they allow heat to escape

habitat: a natural setting in which a species or set of species can live

hot spot: a place with unusually rich biodiversity

megafauna: large animals

natural selection: the tendency of individuals well suited to their environment to survive and pass their genes on to more offspring, so that those genes live on and tend to define that species in that place

range: the geographical area in which a species or a distinct population of a species lives

species: a kind of living thing. Members of a species can reproduce with each other but usually can't share their genes with members of other species.

systemic: having to do with the whole thing rather than just a part—global rather than local

understory: the lowest level of a forest, near the ground

SOURCE NOTES

30 Odell Shepard, ed., *The Heart of Thoreau's Journals* (New York: Dover Publications, 1961), 157.

39 Edward O. Wilson, *The Diversity of Life* (Cambridge, MA: Harvard University Press, 1992), 14.

48 Charles "Stormy" Mayo, interview with author, May 2000.

48 Ibid., Summer 2005.

55 Richard Leakey and Roger Lewin, *The Sixth Extinction: Patterns of Life and the Future of Humankind* (New York: Doubleday, 1995), 239.

56 Alan Burdick, "When Nature Assaults Itself," *New York Times*, op-ed page, April 22, 2005.

59 John Tuxill, *Losing Strands in the Web of Life: Vertebrate Declines and the Conservation of Biological Diversity* (Washington, DC: Worldwatch Institute, 1998), 36–37.

70 Leakey and Lewin, 61.

77 Bill McKibben, *The End of Nature* (New York: Random House, 1989), 7–8, 47.

79 Robert Socolow, quoted by Elizabeth Kolbert in "The Climate of Man," pt. 3, *New Yorker*, May 9, 2005, 52.

83 Jennifer Ackerman, *Notes from the Shore* (New York: Viking Penguin, 1995), 167.

86 Rachel Carson, *Silent Spring* (New York: Fawcett Crest, 1962), 22.

88 Ken Scarlatelli, interview with author, Spring 2000.

100 Charles "Stormy" Mayo, interview with author, May 2000.

SELECTED BIBLIOGRAPHY

Ackerman, Jennifer. *Notes from the Shore*. New York: Viking Penguin, 1995.

Burdick, Alan. *Out of Eden: An Odyssey of Ecological Invasion*. New York: Farrar, Straus and Giroux, 2005.

Carson, Rachel. *Silent Spring*. New York: Fawcett Crest, 1962.

Kaufman, Les, and Kenneth Mallory, eds. *The Last Extinction*. Cambridge, MA: MIT Press, 1993.

Kolbert, Elizabeth. "The Climate of Man." Pts. 1–3. *New Yorker*, April 25, 2005, 56; May 2, 2005, 64; May 9, 2005, 52.

Leakey, Richard, and Roger Lewin. *The Sixth Extinction: Patterns of Life and the Future of Humankind*. New York: Doubleday, 1995.

McKibben, Bill. *The End of Nature*. New York: Random House, 1989.

Novacek, Michael J., ed. *The Biodiversity Crisis: Losing What Counts*. New York: American Museum of Natural History / New Press, 2001.

Shepard, Odell, ed. *The Heart of Thoreau's Journals*. New York: Dover Publications, 1961.

Tuxill, John. *Losing Strands in the Web of Life: Vertebrate Declines and the Conservation of Biological Diversity*. Washington, DC: Worldwatch Institute, 1998.

Wilson, Edward O. *The Diversity of Life*. Cambridge, MA: Harvard University Press, 1992.

FURTHER READING AND WEBSITES

BOOKS

Agenbroad, Larry, and Lisa Nelson. *Mammoths: Ice-Age Giants.* Minneapolis: Twenty-First Century Books, 2002.

Andryszewski, Tricia. *Walking the Earth: The History of Human Migration.* Minneapolis, Twenty-First Century Books, 2007.

Fleisher, Paul. *Evolution.* Minneapolis: Twenty-First Century Books, 2006.

Hecht, Jeff. *Vanishing Life: The Mystery of Mass Extinctions.* New York: Atheneum, 1993.

Hoyt, Erich. *Extinction A-Z.* Berkeley Heights, NJ: Enslow, 1991.

Lampton, Christopher. *Mass Extinctions: One Theory Why the Dinosaurs Vanished.* Danbury, CT: Franklin Watts, 1986.

Mehling, Randi. *Great Extinctions of the Past.* New York: Chelsea House, 2007.

Patent, Dorothy Hinshaw. *The Challenge of Extinction.* Berkeley Heights, NJ: Enslow, 1991.

Silverstein, Alvin, Virginia Silverstein, and Laura Silverstein Nunn. *Adaptation.* Minneapolis: Twenty-First Century Books, 2008.

———. *Food Chains.* Minneapolis: Twenty-First Century Books, 2008.

———. *Symbiosis.* Minneapolis: Twenty-First Century Books, 2008.

———. *Weather and Climate.* Minneapolis: Twenty-First Century Books, 2008.

WEBSITES

Biodiversity Hotspots
http://www.biodiversityhotspots.org
> This site contains information about hot spots, from the nonprofit organization Conservation International.

CITES
http://www.cites.org
> This is the official website concerning the Convention on International Trade in Endangered Species of Wild Fauna and Flora. Administered by the United Nations Environment Programme, the organization ensures that international trade in specimens of wild animals and plants does not threaten their survival.

IUCN Red List of Threatened Species
http://www.redlist.org
> This website features the IUCN (International Union for Conservation of Nature and Natural Resources) Red List of Threatened Species.

Millennium Ecosystem Assessment
http://www.millenniumassessment.org
> This is the website for the United Nations Millennium Ecosystem Assessment.

Provincetown Center for Coastal Studies
http://www.coastalstudies.org
> Information about marine and coastal ecosystems of the North Atlantic, including whale research and rescue programs, is provided.

UNEP World Conservation Monitoring Centre
http://www.unep-wcmc.org
> The United Nations Environment Programme's World Conservation Monitoring Centre, a clearinghouse for information related to biodiversity, offers this website.

Worldwatch Institute
http://www.worldwatch.org
> The nonprofit Worldwatch Institute offers hundreds of publications related to environmental sustainability.

INDEX

ABOUT THE AUTHOR

Tricia Andryszewski has written more than twenty nonfiction books for children and young adults, including *Walking the Earth: The History of Human Migration*. A native of Pittsburgh, Pennsylvania, and a former resident of New York, New Jersey, Virginia, and Connecticut, she lives in the mountains of western North Carolina, near the Tennessee border.

PHOTO ACKNOWLEDGMENTS

The images in this book are used with permission of: © Mark Rassmussen/Fotolia, p. 2 and background images on pp. 10, 23, 30, 39, 48, 56, 59, 70, 77, 79, 86; Robert L. Anderson, USDA Forest Service, www.forestryimages.org, p. 6 (both); Connecticut Agricultural Experimentation Station Archive, Connecticut Agricultural Experimentation Station, www.forestryimages.org, p. 9; Michael Montgomery, USDA Forest Service, www.forestryimages.org, p. 9 (inset); © The Natural History Museum/Alamy, p. 11; © Publiphoto/Photo Researchers, Inc., p. 14; © Javier Etcheverry/Alamy, p. 17 (left); © Ken Lucas/Visuals Unlimited, p. 17 (right); © PHOTOTAKE, Inc./Alamy, p. 18; Laura Westlund/Independent Picture Service, pp. 19; 75; Mary Evans Picture Library, pp. 20, 24; © NASA/Photo Researchers, Inc., p. 21; © Mark Hallett, p. 26; © JUPITERIMAGES/Agence Images/Alamy, p. 28; © Hulton Archive/Getty Images, pp. 30, 37, 42; © Matt Meadows/Peter Arnold, Inc., pp. 33, 35; © North Wind Picture Archives, p. 34; © Gary Braasch Photography, p. 38; Courtesy of Stuart Pimm, Doris Duke Professor of Conservation Ecology, p. 40; © Patrick Frilet/Rex Features USA, pp. 44, 93 (left); © N. A. S./Photo Researchers, Inc., p. 46; © Andrew J. Martinez/Photo Researchers, Inc., p. 49; © Steven Morello/Peter Arnold, Inc., p. 50; Agricultural Research Service, USDA, p. 54; © Nancy J. Pierce/Photo Researchers, Inc., p. 57; © Photomax Specialist Aquarium Picture Library, p. 59; © Paul Baker, courtesy of the Hawaii Division of Forestry and Wildlife, p. 60; © Gregory G. Dimijian, M.D./Photo Researchers, Inc., p. 62; © Terry Whittaker/Photo Researchers, Inc., p. 66; © Lynn Stone, p. 67; © Arthur Morris/Visuals Unlimited, pp. 69, 100; © Tom McHugh/Photo Researchers, Inc., p. 70; © James Steinberg/Photo Researchers, Inc., p. 72; © Scientifica/NOAA/Visuals Unlimited, p. 78; © Christy Kanis/Stock Connection/Rex Features USA, p. 80; © Fred Bruemmer/Peter Arnold, Inc., p. 82; © Russell C. Hansen/Peter Arnold, Inc., p. 84; © CSU Archive/Everett/Rex Features USA, p. 86; © Dr. William J. Weber/Visuals Unlimited, p. 89; © David Cavagnaro/Visuals Unlimited, p. 90; © NIBSC/Photo Researchers, Inc., p. 93 (right); © Charles Melton/Visuals Unlimited, p. 96; © Ingo Arndt/Naturepl.com, p. 97 (top left); © T.J. Rich/Naturepl.com, p. 97 (top right); © Mark Carwardine/Naturepl.com, p. 97 (bottom left); © Bernard Castelein/Naturepl.com; p. 97 (bottom center); © J. Freund/Peter Arnold, Inc., p. 97 (bottom right).

Cover image courtesy of NOAA Central Library Photo Collection.